*Death by Tumbleweed at*
# THE ROUTE 66 RANCH HOTEL

By

N.C.L. SARNO

Death by Tumbleweed
at the Route 66 Ranch Hotel
Copyright © 2025 N.C.L. Sarno

All rights reserved. No portion of this book may be reproduced in any form or by any means, without the prior written permission of the author.

Death by Tumbleweed at the Route 66 Ranch Hotel is a work of fiction. Names, characters, places, and incidents either are the product of the author's imagination or are used fictitiously. Any resemblance to actual persons, living or dead, organizations, events or locales is entirely coincidental.

Cover by N.C.L. Sarno

KDP ISBN: 979-8294309626

Independently Published

Dedicated to
Keepers of the Wild
for thirty years of providing forever homes to wildlife in need.
On Route 66 in the serene area near Valentine, Arizona, this 175-acre sanctuary is dedicated to caring for abused, neglected, and abandoned wild animals. Lions, wolves, tigers, foxes, and bears who had nowhere else to go have all been welcomed to happily spend their lives at Keepers of the Wild.

Previous Books in the Series

Murder at the Route 66 Ranch Hotel

The Mysterious Shootings at the Route 66 Ranch Hotel

Cruiser Crash at the Route 66 Ranch Hotel

Train Robbers at the Route 66 Ranch Hotel

Night Fall at the Route 66 Ranch Hotel

## Chapter One

"Destiny. No, that's not it. Destiny's Door Knock or Destiny's Calling… something like that." Naiya dismissively waved one hand in the air while using the other to take a sip of wine. "You know how racehorses always have overly strange names."

"No, actually I don't," replied Eve. "I've never been to the Kentucky Derby. At no point has my life included the need for big fashionable hats and crisp white gloves."

"Me neither," said Naiya. "But I have an Uncle Roger who likes to play the ponies. Well… he did before he joined Gamblers Anonymous."

"Isn't that supposed to be, you know, anonymous?"

"Oops," Naiya said before taking another sip of wine and tucking some hair from her Cleopatra style bob behind her ear. Eve loved that she and her friend had become so close that they could speak to each other without thinking. With others, they both knew when and where and to whom to say what, but with each other they could relax and say whatever popped into their heads. "Anyway," Naiya continued, "Destiny's Whatever made headlines in the racing world and with her, her equine psychiatrist Dr. Reid Tolliver."

The two women looked across the wine tasting room at the famous Dr. Tolliver. "And he claims that he just talked the horse into winning?" Eve asked skeptically in a hushed tone.

"I'm sure it's more complicated than that," replied Naiya, "but essentially, yes. Almost immediately after starting to work with this run-of-the-mill filly racehorse he turned her into a winner. A big winner. And he's done it time and time again. I guess you could say he specializes in helping horse athletes get over the— oh, what do they call it in sports?"

"The yips?"

"Yeah. The horse yips!" Naiya laughed. "He has a long list of successful clients. He's worth a fortune. There's a lot of money in horse racing. Oh, but I guess you know that since you know about the Kentucky Derby fashion. Money, money, money. Everyone wants to retain his services. I still can't believe he took Emily's presenter spot. The conference became popular as soon as word got out that Reid Tolliver was coming. He doesn't usually do speaking engagements. Everyone wanted to secure a spot to hear him speak. I actually overbooked a little. I hope that's okay."

"It's your conference, you can do what you want," said Eve as she contemplated what to say next. Since they were speaking of horses, she thought this might be a good time to tell her friend something she had been keeping from her. Eve had kept putting off telling Naiya the news and now time was running out. But she opted to chicken out once again and instead said, "As long as the hotel lobby will be big enough for everyone."

"It'll be tight once everyone arrives tomorrow morning," said Naiya, "but I'll make it work. The bus load of attendees comes in from Sandmat at 8:00 am and will leave at 4:00 pm. It's going to be pretty hectic during conference hours, but I think it'll be fine. Thanks again for letting me have this little meet and greet soiree for the presenters and VIP guests tonight."

"Of course. But technically the wine tasting room is part yours. We went into this wine business together and marketing our NaiEve wines to some swanky horse veterinarians is not a bad idea. I mean, I assume they're swanky if they're VIPs." Eve took a sip of her wine as she looked at the two women fawning over Reid Tolliver and his confident charm. She nodded towards them. "Those two women are not presenters, right? So, they're VIPs?"

"Yes."

"And what makes them VIPs of your equine veterinarian conference?" Eve asked.

"They paid more to secure a room at the hotel instead of having to get bussed in from a motel in Sandmat. And they get to come to this meet and greet. I think those two were motivated by the possibility of spending extra time with Dr. Tolliver and his seemingly magical powers. Oh — I mean Reid. I keep forgetting he asked to be called Reid. Despite his fame and fortune, he's really pretty down to earth. Plus, it's common in these situations for us to drop the 'Dr.' stuff since we are all DVMs — Doctor of Veterinary Medicine."

"I know what a DVM is, I have a friend who's a vet. Remember, Dr. Nadar?" Eve said with a wink. "Dr. Reid Tolliver's story is rather fascinating. I think I'd like to hear what he has to say. I might stand in the back during his presentations. In fact, I might need his expertise."

"Why?"

Eve purposefully ignored Naiya's question and asked her own. "If he's so in demand, how did you get him?"

"I'd rather not say," Naiya replied with a scowl.

"Interesting reaction. Now you have to tell me."

"Burt," Naiya replied quietly.

Eve laughed. "Burt? Dr. Burt Bullock? Your self-proclaimed nemesis? That's quite a favor he did for you considering you've told me that he's determined to destroy your life."

"He is!" Naiya insisted in an angry whisper. "He left his veterinary practice here and moved away. That's why I moved here, why I set up my practice here, my boarding facility, my life! I came here because there was a need for my services. But I've had to work hard to get the trust and respect of these ranchers. They missed their good-ol'-boy vet, Burt. Finally, I won them over, mostly, and now I'm invested. I can't leave. But all of sudden, on a whim, he comes back to the area and steals back my hard-earned clients? It's not fair." Naiya took the last sip of her wine, set down her empty wine glass and crossed her arms to complete her full-body pout.

"Well, now I know why he's here as a complimentary VIP," said Eve. "I was wondering." She looked across the room at the square-jawed, ruggedly handsome subject of their conversation. But she wasn't about to mention the attractiveness of the man that Naiya was hellbent on hating.

"Yeah, I had to give him something," said Naiya. "Plus, I guess he doesn't have a place to live yet so he was happy to be able to stay here at the hotel during the conference. For free. I'm so nice."

"So, why would he have done you this favor?" Eve asked.

"I don't know. To showboat. To prove to everyone that he has connections."

"And how is Burt connected to the racehorse king maker?"

"I don't know," Naiya huffed.

Eve thought it best that Naiya stopped talking about Burt. "And tell me again why you chose to organize this conference?"

"Because I, like you, have a problem confusing more work for fun," Naiya said with a smirk. "That's why we're friends."

"Best friends."

"If you want to get all 12-years-old about it."

"I do," replied Eve with a hearty laugh.

"Fine, but I'm not going to wear one of those half of a broken heart necklaces or anything," Naiya said dryly. "And I didn't plan to organize this conference, I only planned to help my old friend Emily, who was organizing it and leading it as the keynote speaker. She had already arranged for the other speakers but was looking for a good venue in Arizona for some reason. I suggested this place and offered to help with a few things. Next thing I knew, she had a family emergency, and I was suddenly the organizer and had an empty keynote speaker spot to fill. Then Burt called and asked if he could sign up for the conference. I was so annoyed that I tried to get rid of him by telling him it probably wasn't going to happen because of Emily... but then the next day he told me Reid Tolliver agreed to speak and Burt offered to help if I needed anything."

"So, you could have had an assistant, but you turned it down for spite?"

"I wasn't going to have him swoop in and take credit for doing all the work. But I had to let him come to the conference. After all, that's what he wanted."

"He seems like a nice enough guy," Eve suggested.

"He SEEMS nice, but I don't buy it. There's something off about him. I tried being sociable at one point and asking him what he had been up to the last five years and he wouldn't tell me. He got suddenly secretive and changed the subject. I don't trust him," Naiya hissed under her breath before pasting on a smile as the wife of one of the presenters approached. "Hello, Margo."

"Do you have any aged wines?" asked the petite, impeccably dressed and jeweled woman. "These reds are too purple for my taste. Purple is an indication that they are young wines, if you didn't know. Your so-called bartender certainly doesn't."

Naiya's subsequent silence and slow intake of breath

was a sign to Eve that her friend was playing out in her head what she actually wanted to say to Margo and rejecting it as rude. Margo had already proven herself to be a pill. It was evident that the difficult woman would require a full-scale tag-team charm offensive. Eve tagged in. "Yes," Eve said cheerfully, "you are correct. Our house made wines are all young since we are a new winery. But we do have other bottles available from more established wineries that are aged."

The assist had given Naiya time to put on her happy face and fake graciousness, which she did flawlessly as she sweetly said, "I'll help the bartender locate some different choices for you." Naiya then walked Margo over to the bar to Eve's clean-upped horse wrangler playing the part of bartender. Her resident bartender, Bridget, was on vacation, so Eve had begged Wes to fill in. He had conceded to the job since he only had to pour wine and not mix cocktails. But fielding questions about wine was certainly not in his wheelhouse. She had hoped that his unparalleled good looks wrapped up in a bow tie would be so dazzling that the guests would not question his qualifications. Apparently, Margo was undazzled. Not for the first time, Eve questioned her decision to become a winemaker. *People get so weird about wine,* she thought as she shook her head. *Maybe I should have opened a brewery. Craft beer people are more laid back. I wonder if hops grow here. Or I could just move somewhere where hops grow…*

Eve smiled, laughing at herself. As if she could, or would, move. She had spent the last few years of her life dedicated to creating this rural hotel-restaurant-horse riding- vineyard-winery business. Just like Naiya, Eve was invested. She couldn't leave. Luckily, she didn't want to. She loved her life here in rural northern Arizona.

Her happy thoughts quickly darkened. She suddenly became genuinely worried about Dr. Burt (as he liked to go by) and his arrival back to the area. What if he did get all of his old clients back and Naiya couldn't afford to keep her business? What if she moved? Eve couldn't handle the idea and quickly purged it from her mind. She distracted herself with the entertainment as old as humanity: people watching.

She focused on presenter Arthur (or Art) Wells, husband of the wine snob Margo Wells. Eve had met him earlier and had liked him immediately. Art was a soft-spoken, medium built, middle-aged man that would be hard to pick out of a crowd. But once you talked to him, it was evident that he was an interesting and kind man—a man who was far too nice for his wife in Eve's opinion. She wondered if Art and Margo had simply become different people as their marriage had grown long in the tooth. It wouldn't be the first time she had seen young love sour as it aged. She secretly used examples such as these to justify her decision to not marry at a young age. Of course, now that she had just turned forty, she wondered if she had waited too long. But being happily single was far better than being unhappily hitched, she reminded herself as she looked at Art. Art was tucked in the corner having a quiet but intense conversation with conference VIP Jessica Denmon. Jessica, who appeared to be in her early thirties, was as graceful in her movements as she was professional in her appearance. She wore a white, silk, long-sleeved blouse and dark rimmed glasses that matched her dark hair which she wore in a tight bun.

Eve then looked again at the ladies that were chatting up Reid Tolliver. She couldn't remember their names, so she snuck a peak at the hotel guest sheet she had printed out and put in her pocket. By process of elimination, she determined they must be Kelly Cheesborough and Sheila Kamnitz. Eve was pretty sure that Sheila was the one who kept finding reasons to pat the famous Dr. Reid Tolliver on the arm.

Speakers Olive Hudson and Gabriel Spurlock were standing in the middle of the room having a spirited professional conversation about understanding the risk of intra-articular medication in racehorses. At least, that was what Eve had attempted to deduce during the loud, technical conversation that dominated the room. Eve saw both Reid's and Art's concentration in their own conversations get distracted multiple times. As they discussed their work, Olive, wearing a tweed blazer, theatrically waved her arms while Gabriel conservatively pulled on the chin hairs of his trim black beard. Although almost completely opposite in physical appearance — Olive was short, stout, with white hair, while Gabriel was tall, lean, with black hair — Eve thought they both looked like ivy league college professors.

Naiya's new rival, Burt, was having a relaxed, pleasant conversation with Colin McCullough, another hotel guest/VIP. Eve loved that the fact that getting to stay at her hotel was what made them VIPs. Only very important people got to stay at her very important place. Eve studied Burt Bullock to see if she could discern an evil agenda on his weatherworn face. She didn't. But she could understand why the local ranchers might have a connection with Dr. Burt. He looked more like a cowboy than a veterinarian. The only thing marring his rough and tumble country boy persona was the comfortable way he held his delicate wine glass. Colin looked like a slightly older version of Burt. Eve thought it funny that the professor lookalikes and the cowboy lookalikes had gravitated to each other.

Finally, she focused her attentions on speaker Lorenzo Dominguez who was talking with VIP Henry Bayless. Eve was sure that 'Latin' and 'lover' were the two words that popped into anyone's mind when they first looked at the handsome horse trainer based out of the affluent Scottsdale area on the outskirts of Phoenix. Lorenzo's almost constant smile showed off dimples and perfect teeth. His easy stance boasted an athletic build and perfect posture. And then, there was his absolutely perfect skin. She was sure that as a horse trainer he must spend a lot of time outside, but the elements hadn't done him any harm. Obviously, the brutal Arizona sun didn't hurt Lorenzo, it loved him. His skin soaked it up during the day and then shone out of him at night. The longer Eve looked at him, the more magnificent he appeared.

"Dibs," said Naiya's voice quietly and closely behind Eve's head.

Eve turned around with a smile. "Not fair!"

"Dibs. Dibs. Dibs," Naiya said slowly as she joined in the pleasant task of looking at Lorenzo. "I didn't ask him to be a presenter just to get butts in the seats. I also wanted his butt up here."

"Naiya!"

"What? Look at it! I'm only human," she sighed. "And if I didn't say it before— dibs."

"Wait— I thought Emily picked all the presenters."

"She did but then she realized everyone was from her part of the world in Kentucky. She thought if she was having a conference in Arizona, she should have at least one presenter from Arizona. I suggested Lorenzo. I had seen him at a conference in Phoenix."

"He's not a veterinarian though. Is everyone going to be alright having a non-vet speaker?"

"I hope so. He's not here for eye candy purposes only. He's an exceptional horse trainer. He has a superior reputation for calming excitable horses. I'm sure that all vets could use his advice in learning how to deal with difficult horses. It's an important lesson, whomever it comes from."

"Hmmmm," Eve murmured as she looked thoughtfully at the horse trainer.

"Hmmmm, what?"

Eve looked at her friend guiltily. She shook it off and said, "Did you find Margo an acceptable wine? It's too bad that Bridget isn't here to bartend. But on the bright side, at least our perpetual-pain vintner isn't here to look down his nose at everyone."

"Where is Giancarlo again? I know you told me, but I've been preoccupied."

"He and Dean are gone for a few days doing a supply run and looking at available irrigation upgrades." Eve was still in awe at how her day and night wine-making team got along. Her sweet young grape grower and her old cranky wine maker worked together so well. She didn't understand it but didn't question it. She always reminded herself not to look a gift horse in the mouth. As the phrase "gift horse" swirled around in her head, her previous guilty expression reappeared.

"What's going on?" asked Naiya. "I feel like there's something you're not telling me.

"You've been busy," Eve began apologetically. "I haven't wanted to bother you with it. But it is something that is going to affect you… and you might be upset with me. And I guess I should tell you because I just found out that I need to take him sooner than later."

"What are you talking about?"

"I'm getting a new horse."

"That's fine. I can handle one more horse to my workload. Especially with Burt stealing clients from me."

"It's a special horse."

"Special?"

"He has problems."

"No!" Naiya said with the wide eyes of realization. "Not that horse?"

Eve looked apologetically at her friend and nodded.

"Blaze?" Naiya asked.

"Yes, Blaze."

"You're the one taking him?"

"Someone has to. They're dropping him off tomorrow."

Naiya sighed. "Then you better clean up tumbleweeds all night."

## Chapter Two

When Eve first drove the lonely 30-mile stretch of Route 66 from the closest town of Sandmat out to her inherited hotel and old ranch property, a tumbleweed had blown across the road in front of her. She had squealed with delight at the western welcome. But as time went on, Eve's love of tumbleweeds diminished swiftly and severely. At first, she thought an occasional tumbleweed blowing across a field was cute and westerny but admitted that piles of them along the fence line looked dirty and unkempt. When Eve learned that tumbleweeds were introduced to the United States from illegally imported wheat seed from Russia in the mid-1800s and that one tumbleweed scatters 200,000 seeds as it rolls across the land, she really started to dislike them. Then, after finding out firsthand that the spikey thorns on the spherical dried weeds were incredibly painful, she started to hate them. And finally, when attempting tumbleweed herding on a windy day she found that a tumbleweed's need for speed and unpredictability made her look a fool, that's when she vowed complete destruction. She was now bound and determined to take down Big Tumbleweed.

Her employees were well aware that Eve strived to

make her property a tumbleweed-free zone. Therefore, gathering tumbleweeds was something that everyone on the staff did regularly. Just off the road on the way to the staff cabins, Wes constructed a pen with an extra high privacy fence to keep the weeds contained and out of sight. All the staff members helped in transferring any of the roaming weeds to the pen. Eve called this the "Tumbleweed Relocation Program."

A few of her guests, who were visiting the area and were under the misapprehension that the weeds were charming, had requested to take a tumbleweed home with them. One lady recently sent her a picture of her tumbleweed statue that was simply a tumbleweed collected from the Route 66 Ranch Hotel that had been spray painted gold. But for every crazy person that wanted a tumbleweed souvenir from their southwest excursion, there were hundreds more to destroy.

When the pen got full, the group of hotel employees had discussed at length how to dispose of the growing mountain of intertwined wispy yet formidable spikey spheres. Most suggested burning, and they tried it once, but Eve couldn't stand the smell and unsightliness. She eventually gave in to Wes's suggestion that they get a small woodchipper. It sounded horribly dangerous to Eve, but she set aside her tendency to be overly cautious and finally conceded. If that was what Wes thought would make the tiresome chore of tumbleweed destruction entertaining for him, she'd buy him a woodchipper. Men like the strangest toys.

Due to her staff's dedication to see Eve's dream realized, the Route 66 Ranch Hotel property had become known as a tumbleweed free property. Strangely, this is what precipitated the recent offer of a free horse.

Eve was anxious about the arrival of her new horse. She woke up extra early, and after her walk with her dog, Sunset, and Naiya's dog, the adorable slobber beast named Midas, whom she had volunteered to look after during the conference, she led them out to the stables to see Wes. Wes was a habitual early riser, and he was there as expected. Eve got straight to the point and asked Wes if she had made a rash decision agreeing to take in the problem horse.

He quickly attempted to alleviate her fears. "It'll be fine," Wes said with conviction.

"It's not as if we are completely tumbleweed free," Eve argued. "They blow in from everywhere. Sure, we're good about cleaning them up when we see them, but we can't guarantee that Blaze is never going to see one. I can't believe I have yet another reason to hate tumbleweeds."

"He's really a very nice horse," Wes assured her. "He only freaks out if a tumbleweed is blowing right at him or is right under his feet. If one is against the horse pasture fence in the distance, he'll be fine."

"But when he has… an episode… it's pretty bad, right?"

"I guess so. I haven't seen it but they're giving him to you for free for a reason."

"They're giving him to us. You're going to be the one who takes care of him. I don't want to be putting you in a dangerous situation."

"I'll be fine," Wes said. "He'll be fine, I'll be fine, and you'll be fine. If there's any problems, we'll deal with them. We've dealt with a lot worse. We can handle it. They couldn't use him for cowboying purposes, but he'll be fine here with us. We'll give him the special treatment he needs."

"But they're sending someone from animal control to witness the transfer of the potentially dangerous animal. Doesn't that worry you?"

"It's just legal stuff. He had a fit and someone called it in. Now the poor horse is on a watchlist. Blaze had a bad day and someone called the cops on him. It's happened to me before, remember? That bad moment shouldn't define him. Everything'll be fine."

Wes's unwavering confidence reassured her. She reminded herself that the horse needed a home, and this was by far his best option in the tumbleweed infested area. She walked out of the building and nervously scanned the property, making sure it was still tumbleweed free. Luckily, it was not windy today. The often-relentless springtime wind could not deliver any. They were safe, for now.

She also reminded herself that she had a hotel full of horse experts. She could not waste that opportunity. She would consult with at least one of them about the problems of her soon-to-be ward.

Eve often left Sunset with Wes for the day and Wes didn't mind taking Midas as well. The two dogs loved playing with each other so much they would entertain themselves.

She returned to the hotel to help Naiya prepare for the conference, or rather, she attempted to help. She tried to help set up the conference space in the lobby, but all the jobs were already spoken for. Loretta and Roxie were arranging the many padded folding chairs and Ramon was on audio visual duty setting up the display screen and wireless microphones. Ramon loved figuring out the latest technologies. Anytime they got a new piece of electronic equipment, Eve relied on Ramon to read the manual, learn the intricacies and then teach her. Eve went to the kitchen to see if Esperanza needed any help preparing the coffee and breakfast buffet for the guests or the morning snacks for the conference but, of course, she didn't. Sometimes Eve wondered if her employees were going to realize that she was superfluous to this organization. Luckily, the phone rang at the reception desk and she was able to run across the lobby and look busy.

After booking a reservation, Eve saw Naiya exit the downstairs Suite C that she was staying in during the 3-day conference. She walked towards Eve at the front desk looking more than a little frazzled and wiping her nose with a tissue. "Hey," she said to Eve, "I haven't had a chance to get those spare keys for the winery made yet. Sorry."

"That's okay," said Eve with concern. "But that's not a priority right now. You have other, more pressing matters to attend to."

"I know, I know," said Naiya. "Why did Emily insist on having this conference in northern Arizona? Sorry. I'm a bit flustered right now. I just found out that Cheryl is quitting."

"Your office manager? Isn't she the one who takes care of the boarding facility most of the time?"

"Yes. I don't know how I'm going to replace her. It's due to a family emergency so she's leaving right after the conference is over. Can you believe it? Another family emergency? Emily and now Cheryl. People around me are dropping like flies. And to top it off, Cheryl rents the cabin on my property. So, I'm out that rental income as well as my main employee. And I'm thinking of all the things I have to do and how I'm going to be able to do them without her, like making those keys. And just to make things more fun, my allergies are killing me. I—" Naiya cut off her slightly frantic rant as she became distracted by the sound of doors opening and closing on the upstairs balcony. "Looks like people are ready for breakfast. Time to be a good hostess."

"You go do whatever you need to do," said Eve. "Let me be hostess. It's my job, my only job it seems. I'm a little bored. I'll take care of the hotel guests. You take care of the conference."

"Thanks. I do want to call the bus driver and make sure that everything is on schedule." Naiya circled around the room checking in with Ramon, Loretta, and Roxie before disappearing back into her suite.

Eve made her way to the dining room to play hostess. At the party last night, she had eventually made the rounds and introduced herself to each of her guests.

"Do you mind if I join you all for a cup of coffee?" Eve asked the group.

"That would be delightful," replied Art. "Let me get one for you. How do you take it?"

"Cream, no sugar," Eve said. While Art darted off to the breakfast buffet on the bar, Eve turned to Margo. "Your husband is so nice."

"Yes," Margo replied drily. "So nice he'll gladly give you the shirt off my back." She shot the back of her husband's head a dirty look as she added, "And the cup of coffee he should have offered to make for me."

From the coffee station, Art turned and said, "I never make it the right way and you always complain and make yourself a new cup anyway."

"You could just learn how to do it correctly," Margo projected so that her husband, and everyone else could hear her. The closest eardrum took the brunt of the loud bickering. Eve rubbed her ringing ear as she watched Margo walk away to make her own coffee.

Last night, Eve had learned that the famous Reid Tolliver was a flirt, particularly with her. She was not surprised when he took the opportunity to immediately replace Margo's spot next to her. He smiled and started to say something when a sneeze overtook him. His body shuddered, violently relieving him of his come-hither gaze. After the sneeze, he automatically wiped his nose on the sleeve of his cashmere cardigan.

"For heaven's sake, Reid! Don't do that!" Margo barked. "Use a tissue, like a grown up," she added as she pulled one from her expensive-looking handbag and thrust it towards him.

Reid succeeded in keeping a neutral expression as he took the proffered tissue, but Eve could tell that it was forced. She didn't think Reid was used to being spoken to like a misbehaving child.

Art quickly handed Eve her cup of coffee and walked

away, sitting at a table with Colin. Reid looked at Eve and simply said, "Allergies," before he changed the subject to the work he was having done on his chalet in Aspen.

Eve only half listened to Reid as she eavesdropped on the conversation between Art and Colin.

Colin was saying, "It's such a good program. I'm sure you'll change your mind when you see it."

"I'm sure it is," replied Art. "And I'm happy to come take a tour but I can't personally help you right now. I don't have that kind of money. Maybe in a year. Who knows? We'll see how things pan out. But right now, I just can't do it. I'm sorry."

"But…" Colin began with trepidation. "You still… you know, made provisions for the organization?"

"Yes, I did, for the future. But right now, I can't do anything. But, like I said, I'm happy to tour the facility and tell others about it. I'll do what I can."

Eve was paying just enough attention to Reid to realize that he had asked her the question, "Do you ski?"

"Ski?" she echoed, buying herself a little time as she reverted her full attention to Reid. "Oh, I've thrown myself down a bunny hill or two, but I wouldn't call it skiing. I learned pretty quickly that I prefer looking at the snow rather than falling into it face first and eating it. Admiring the snow from the safety of a nice warm lodge is my thing."

"My chalet is perfect for that," Reid replied with a twinkle in his eye.

"Speaking of snow," said Jessica. "It's cold enough out there to snow. Do you ever get snow in the early spring here?"

"Oh yes," said Eve. "It's possible. I should probably check the weather."

"I live and die by my weather app," Reid said to Jessica in his smoothest of voices. "Let me check it for you." He shot Jessica a toothy smile as he pulled out his phone.

Jessica rolled her eyes and walked away.

Eve and Reid's faces mirrored each other with confusion, but before either of them could comment on Jessica's strange behavior, Margo reappeared and, as usual, demanded all the attention be directed to her. "Where is your business center?" Margo asked Eve.

"We don't have one," replied Eve. "What do you need?"

Margo huffed with exasperation. "I need to print something. My brilliant…" she paused to let the word 'brilliant' hang in the air to emphasize that she had said it dripping with sarcasm, "husband forgot to print out his presentations."

"You can use the printer in my office," Eve said trying to mask her discomfort at the prospect of spending any alone time with Margo. Just then Roxie walked into the room and Eve pounced on the opportunity to pawn Margo off on her. Eve felt a little guilty, but Roxie was young and resilient. She could handle it, Eve told herself. Much like the raising of children, the handling of high maintenance people took a village. After asking Roxie to help Margo get her things printed in the office, Eve once again found herself in conversation with Reid and once again found herself distracted. She felt too guilty about throwing Roxie to the wolves. After a few minutes, she politely excused herself and went to the office.

Her worries were unfounded. Roxie was staring at her phone giggling at something while Margo watched a piece of paper finish printing.

"Finally!" said Margo as she scooped up a pile of papers. "Your printer is so slow."

Eve's printer was brand new and top of the line. She knew that it was not slow. Margo was just one of those people who didn't know how to say something that wasn't a complaint. Eve found Margo's behavior infuriating, but she told herself that Margo should be pitied not hated. What a sad way to live your life trying to make yourself feel better by constantly putting down every person and every piece of innocent office machinery.

Margo stormed out due to the injustices of the fictional slow printing that she was pretending she had to endure. Eve thanked Roxie, who nodded and left. She went to the printer to add paper and was annoyed to find that it had been full of her nice heavyweight cream-colored paper that she used to print menu inserts. Eve knew it was a stupid thing to get upset about, but Margo had just used up almost all of her good paper! Eve could be magnanimous about Margo's awful personality but when it came to her good paper…

Eve started laughing out loud and was happy that no one was there to witness her spurt of crazy. *It's just paper!* she reminded herself. She filled up her printer with the cheap stuff and got online to order more of the menu insert paper. Plus, it was for Art, not Margo. Art deserved to have nice paper for his presentations.

That made Eve feel better. A little better. She still had a bad taste in her mouth from having to deal with Margo. Eve knew that the next few days were going to be much more challenging because of that lady. There was no doubt about it. Margo Wells was going to be trouble.

## Chapter Three

While working quietly on the front desk computer, Eve listened to most of the conference's morning presentations. She thought the conference was running very smoothly and could tell Naiya was relaxing more and more with every successful presentation. But just before lunch when something did go wrong, Eve felt she had jinxed it.

While Gabriel was finishing his presentation on the elaborate array of horse hoof conditions and how to treat them (which seemed to be fascinating to the audience of veterinarians but was giving Eve a new and intense paranoia of all the possible problems that might happen to her cherished horses) the microphone went out. Ramon, on-deck as amateur tech support, ran around trying to fix it to no avail. But it was no emergency. Gabriel was quite comfortable raising his voice to reach the back row. His pompous tendency to speak over everyone else actually came in handy.

After the presentation, Naiya and Ramon huddled and spoke in hushed voices. As directed by Esperanza, the conference attendees slowly made their way to the dining room for the lunch spread. Eve noticed that Margo had appeared in the lobby and was hanging back, keeping her eye on Naiya.

"I'll go out to my car and get it," Naiya said to Ramon and went into her suite.

Margo moved to the front door. Naiya returned from her suite and handed a box to Ramon. Margo once again crossed the room, this time with her hands parked on the hips of her stylish dark brown dress.

"I thought you were going outside to your car," Margo said to Naiya in an irritated tone. "I was waiting at the front door for you!"

"Oh, sorry," Naiya said distractedly to Margo as she pointed to an electronic device in the box to bring it to Ramon's attention. "I have an external door in my suite that goes out to the parking lot. I used that."

"Well, you should have said that," Margo huffed.

Naiya looked at Margo pleasantly. Eve expected only she, being Naiya's good friend, was able to tell that Naiya was masking her intense annoyance. "What did you need, Margo?" Naiya asked sweetly.

"I want to know if it's going to snow," replied Margo. "The weather says it might snow. Well, my weather app says it's going to snow. The one Art uses says nothing about it. You live here. Is it going to snow? I don't want to get stuck out here."

"Snow?" Naiya said with a chuckle. "I'll believe it when I see it," said Naiya. "A few weeks ago, they said there was going to be a big snowstorm and we all planned for it and then nothing happened. So, no, I don't think so. I wouldn't worry about it."

Margo scrunched her eyebrows together, pursed her lips, and stared at Naiya disbelievingly for a few beats before she unceremoniously walked away and headed upstairs to her room, Suite B.

As soon as Margo had loudly closed the door behind her, it was Naiya's turn to be huffy. She looked at Eve, letting her real emotions take hold of her facial expression. "Nothing I do seems to satisfy that woman! Now I'm in trouble for using my conveniently placed side door instead of the front door? Come on!"

"Why is she here?" Ramon asked as he continued his work fixing the microphone.

"I wondered the same thing," said Eve. "She doesn't seem to be enjoying herself. Why would she come on this trip?"

"Who knows!" said Naiya. "I for one wish she hadn't. She has nothing to do with the conference, but she is taking up half of my time. Everyone would be better off if she would have just stayed home."

"I agree," said Eve. "But I don't know if I agree with you about the weather. I was talking to a Sandmat old-timer in town last week and—"

"Old-timer?" Naiya interrupted with a laugh.

"Yes, that is what he referred to himself as and I like it. So, this old-timer said that every time there's an unseasonably warm winter, like we had this year, there is always a big spring snowstorm."

"I've lived here too long to get taken in by the folksy country lore," said Naiya.

"Do not underestimate the insight of a Sandmat old-timer," said Ramon. "We know things."

"Please!" Eve laughed. "You've got another twenty years before you dip your toe into the pool of old-timer."

"I can't wait." Ramon paused his work and with a faraway look said, "The townspeople will all gather around me to hear my words of wisdom. I will impart knowledge of long ago. I will tell the children of the horrors we had to overcome, like T.V. antennas."

Eve giggled as she walked away to let Naiya and Ramon finish fixing the conference's audio system and went into the dining room to check out the lunch spread. Eve stood next to Olive at the trays of sandwiches.

"What kind of cheese is on that sandwich?" Olive

asked Eve with a finger pointed at one of the trays.

"Provolone, I think," said Eve.

"Alright. As long as it's not American."

"Oh no. We don't have American cheese here."

"Good. I'm not a culinary master or anything but I know two things: If it's white, it isn't chocolate, and if it's 'American' it isn't cheese."

"That sounds unpatriotic," said Gabriel.

"No," replied Olive. "Whoever named that plastic goo was unpatriotic. How dare they associate our great country with that abomination." Jessica laughed as she put a sandwich on her plate, which directed Olive's attention towards her. "Jessica, you look so familiar to me. Have we met?"

"No, I don't think so," replied Jessica as she finished getting her lunch together. "But we can do it now. Would you like to have lunch with me?"

"Sure!" Olive replied with a smile. "That's an exceedingly kind invitation. Fair warning, yes, I do have a lot of opinions about a lot of things, but please know that for every one of them that I say out loud, I do have the decency to keep about twenty more to myself."

Eve wandered around the crowded room making sure that everyone had what they needed and as she did, she listened in on snippets of conversations of her hotel guests. She thought it was funny how she instinctually tuned out the chatter of the other conference attendees and directed her attentions primarily to the overnight guests at her hotel. Her role of hotel owner had taken over the better part of her personality. *Maybe I need to get my own social life!* she considered but quickly discarded the thought as she once again focused on her eavesdropping. She heard Art and Colin having a similar conversation to the one she had heard at breakfast about Colin's horse sanctuary. She listened in on Lorenzo and Henry's conversation about the importance of quality horse saddles. She heard Jessica mention her four-year-old son and asked Olive if she had kids. Olive said, "No. I never had children. Apparently, it's only my mind that's fertile." This won her another of Jessica's delightful laughs.

Roxie came in holding a pitcher of water and walked to the bar. "Aren't you going to eat?" she asked Eve as she poured the water into the countertop dispenser.

"No, I'm trying to eat less. I'm getting a little too... um... Rubenesque."

"What does that mean?" asked Roxie.

"It means she's been eating too many Reuben sandwiches," answered Olive with what could only be described as a hoot.

"It does?" Roxie looked suspiciously at Olive.

Eve laughed. "While that's not entirely untrue, no, that is not what that means."

"Whatever," Roxie said, unbothered, as she walked away.

"You look fantastic," Olive said to Eve. "Take it from someone who is actually Rubenesque and truly thankful for the Baroque paintings of Peter Paul Rubens for attempting to make my full-figured kind fashionable—you are a wee slip of a thing."

"Thank you, but my scale and I are in a fight right now."

"Oh, you don't have to tell me about that. My scale and I have been at it for years. I've called it a dirty liar more than once. In fact, one time I was so desperate for it to go down just a little, I blew my nose and got back on the scale hoping that it would tip it in my favor. It did not." Olive belted out a laugh. "But listen, if you have recently put on a little weight, it's a good sign. It means you are ready for love."

"Oh really? How is that?"

"Love can't take hold of you unless you have the appropriate handles."

Eve laughed. "Olive, thank you! I was looking for the

most tenuous excuse to not skip lunch. And that works for me!" Eve grabbed a sandwich and a bag of chips before sitting to eat with Olive and Jessica. She waved Naiya over to join them when she finally came in to eat.

Shortly after the conference resumed after the lunch break, Eve got a text from Wes with news that Blaze was on his way. She made her way out to the horse pasture and nervously waited with Wes. When the expected vehicles arrived, she was taken aback.

Eve had prepared for her new horse's arrival, but she hadn't prepared for Sheriff Strider's arrival. She was perplexed when she saw that the horse trailer was being followed by a Juniper County Sheriff's Department SUV. When she realized it was Sheriff Strider's vehicle, she automatically smoothed down her hair and tried to ignore that her heart had started beating just a little bit faster.

When the sheriff exited his vehicle, Eve tried to sound nonchalant as she said, "What are you doing here? I thought someone from animal control was coming."

"It's a big county in size but small in population and resources. The sheriff's department wears many hats. Today, I wear the hat of animal control officer."

"Oh, so, you're like a multi-talented hero."

He raised an eyebrow. "I wouldn't use the word 'like.'"

If Eve had something she was going to say, she couldn't remember. She couldn't stop giggling.

As Wes and Clay, the neighboring cowboy who had brought Blaze, started making the move to let Blaze out into the pasture, Eve forced herself to stop noticing how handsome the sheriff looked and focused on the task at hand. She again nervously scanned the area for tumbleweeds. Still clear.

Blaze exited the trailer with no drama whatsoever. The sleek, strong, young, mahogany brown American Saddlebred easily joined the other horses in the pasture.

Eve let out a sigh of relief. "See. No cause for alarm," she said to the sheriff. "He's not a bad animal."

"I never said he was," he replied kindly. "After a call comes in reporting that an animal might be dangerous, we simply need to be cautious. I'm here to protect. If anything ever happens with him, if you think he's dangerous, you need to call me. Your safety is my priority."

She held onto those last few words while he walked over to speak to Clay. Wes came to Eve.

"I like him," said Wes as he admired Blaze taking in his new surroundings.

"Me too," Eve agreed. "What a stunning sensitive soul, if perhaps too sensitive. But that just makes me want to take care of him even more."

"We will," he said.

Eve could tell that Wes felt equally drawn to the beautiful animal.

After Clay drove off with the empty horse trailer and Wes went to spend some quality time with Blaze, Sheriff Strider returned to Eve.

"I heard that Roy moved," he said directly but awkwardly.

"He… I… Yeah… He did," she replied not so directly and much more awkwardly.

"So, does that mean you're not dating anymore?"

"I… Yeah. I mean, I don't know that we were 'dating.' We went on some dates… a few dates, but we weren't dating," she said without an ounce of grace, realizing how stupid that sounded. "Well… Nothing much ever came of it and then he decided to move. So, yeah, I'm not dating Roy."

"Okay," he said with slight smile.

"Or anyone," she added pathetically. "I'm not dating anyone."

His smile broadened as his phone rang and remained on his face while he took the short phone call. After hanging up, he said, "Duty calls."

"Who's Duty? Is she pretty?"

"No," he laughed. "Definitely not."

"It was nice seeing you. It's been too long."

"I'm glad you think so. You know, I don't usually work the animal control calls. I usually farm those out to my deputies."

"Oh. Well, I'm glad you came on this one."

"Me too."

When she returned to the conference, she had to consciously stop herself from smiling as she quietly snuck in the back and listened to the end of Reid Tolliver's presentation on "Equine Psychiatry: Knowing When to Pivot."

He was saying, "Often when trying to solve a problem, you come up with a plan, plotting every step meticulously, down to the slightest detail, and then BOOM: a different and better solution presents itself. What do most people do in this situation? They stick with their original plan. Why? Because they value their time so much they don't want it to be wasted. They hate the idea that they spent all those hours planning, working, calculating. They can't stand the idea that all that time constructing the perfect solution was all for naught. So, they stick with plan A. They prioritize planning over success, they choose strategy over inspiration.

"The key to my success is accepting that my first idea was wrong and moving on. Nine times out of ten something happens, something changes direction and I choose to follow that new path. I simply accept a workable solution when it presents itself to me. My successful strategy is knowing when to pivot."

When Reid asked for questions at the end of his presentation, Eve told herself that even though Blaze's arrival went smoothly, she should still take advantage of the magnitude of knowledge in the room and present the case of Blaze's troubles. She didn't expect the contentious debate that followed.

After explaining Blaze's extreme reaction to the sight of tumbleweed, everyone had something to say on the subject. None of it was particularly helpful, Eve thought. But as the conversation continued, opinions became more fevered. Eventually, everyone dropped out of the hot debate as Art and Gabriel went head to head. Eve thought it was almost as if Gabriel was purposefully provoking Art. Every time Art said something, Gabriel swatted something contradictory back at him. As if it was a tennis match, the heads of the crowd swung back and forth as they looked from Art, and then to Gabriel, back to Art, and then back to Gabriel. Everyone's heads moved in unison, except for Eve's and Jessica's. Eve's head stayed still as she kept her focus on Jessica who was keeping her gaze firmly planted on Art.

"Intense immersion therapy?" said Art. "That's your suggestion?"

"Yes," Gabriel said, pompous as ever. "You need to put a tumbleweed right in his face and let him get it out of his system."

"Your suggestion is to scare the poor animal to death? You'd likely give him a heart attack before you cured his fear!"

"You have to be tough in situations like these," Gabriel said, bearded chin in the air.

"Tough? Tough? Ha!" Art replied. "We are doctors. Horses are our patients. It is not our job to be tough. Tough kills."

"Is that a dig on the horse racing industry? I know you have a problem with it."

"I— I have concerns about it, just like anyone should. When animals are put into positions where people make money off of them—"

"Don't we all make money off of animals?" Gabriel said.

"You are getting off topic," Art said as he took a deep

breath and directed his gaze at Eve. He calmly continued by telling her, "I am confident that intensive immersion therapy is not the correct plan of treatment for your new horse. For right now, you simply need to establish trust with this horse and keep the tumbleweeds away from him to the best of your ability. Let him experience this new home as a safe space. There is an incredibly good probability that the problem goes away on its own as Blaze gets older and wiser. If it doesn't, you are more than welcome to call me and I will help you come up with a plan."

Eve thanked everyone for their suggestions before making herself scarce. She didn't want to create any more disturbances. Plus, sometimes people overwhelmed her. Too many personalities, too many problems. She felt like spending time with the simple and pure souls of the dogs and the horses. Comparing Blaze's tumbleweed problem with the intense and varied problems of humans put it in perspective. It really didn't seem so bad.

It never occurred to her what might happen if her new horse's problem was coupled with a problem of a particularly horrible human.

# Chapter Four

As soon as the conference had come to its conclusion for the day, Eve made her way through the crowd to find Naiya. She apologized for her earlier interruption.

Naiya surprised her by saying, "Are you kidding? It was great! These conferences can be kind of dry sometimes. And despite Reid Tolliver's famous results, I thought his presentation was a little underwhelming. The group discussion really spiced things up."

"I wasn't all that impressed with his talk either. Of course, I only walked in at the end, but still, I was hoping that in it he would give some useful information, but I didn't hear any. It seemed pretty vague. That's why I felt the need to ask a question. But I get it, I'm sure he doesn't want to give away his trade secrets."

"Yes, but these conferences are to share information so that we can be better vets. The well-being of the animals should come before personal gain. Of course," she added with a laugh, "I say that as someone who has nothing to lose."

Eve followed Naiya out the front door as she ushered everyone staying in Sandmat to load themselves on the bus. As Naiya directed the foot traffic, Art joined her and they both thanked the attendees for coming to the conference and said they looked forward to seeing them tomorrow. As Eve, Art, and Naiya waved goodbye to the bus as it drove down the driveway, Eve noticed that some of the other presenters and VIPs had also come outside to see the bus off.

Olive was walking by talking to Sheila, "I still need to iron out my presentation for tomorrow morning. I reread it and it's not as polished as I thought it was. I thought I was golden, but I'm bronze at best."

Naiya elbowed Eve and said, "Bronze at Best, good pub name."

Eve nodded and smiled until she saw something that swiftly wiped the joy from her heart and the smile from her face. The wind had picked up and she saw that a tumbleweed was blowing towards them. After discussing Blaze's condition with everyone at the conference, Eve was not the only one who had a severe reaction to the sight.

"Oh no!" Olive cried as she pointed to the large weed heading towards Reid and Gabriel. When it arrived to the two men, they both simply side stepped out of the way of its path. Olive and Colin, on the other hand, both scrambled towards the menacing orb like it was a fumbled football. "Ow," said Colin when he captured it and was rewarded with scratches all over his uncovered arms.

"Thank you!" Eve exclaimed to Olive and Colin. "You are so kind. I have an interim tumbleweed pen over here by the laundry room. I can take it," she said to Colin as she reached for the extra-large weed.

"No, I'll keep it," said Colin. "No point in you getting scratched up as well. I'm okay. I'm used to cleaning up tumbleweeds at my horse sanctuary in Yarnell. Just lead the way, I'll follow you." As they walked, he said, "One time my keys fell into a tumbleweed before a gust of wind blew it away. I chased it for a quarter of a mile before I caught the bugger. I learned that once you have one in your hands, it's best not to let go!"

When they arrived at the small square of wire fencing, Eve noticed it was empty. Wes must have cleaned it out today and took the other weeds to the big pen. "You can just toss it in here," she said to Colin. "Sorry about the scratches."

"Not a problem. My fault for wearing a short-sleeved shirt when it's this cold," he said jovially.

Colin and Eve talked about the possibility of snow as they walked back to join Art and Naiya.

"Disaster averted," Eve said lightheartedly, trying to hide her previous panic. She was wondering if she was going to be able to survive this new horse. Blaze's affliction was already becoming hers. She was starting to have anxious fits at the sight of tumbleweeds.

"I'm still giving Blaze his exam at 5:00, right?" Naiya asked Eve.

"Yes. Wes said he'll put him in a stable for you but take your time. I think Wes is enjoying spending some quality time with our new adoptee."

"Okay, sounds good. I'd like to decompress and shake off my role as conference organizer before resuming my role as local vet."

"Great. I'll meet you out there at 5:00."

Naiya left and Colin followed her into the hotel. Eve was about to remind Art that dinner service started at 6:00, but she didn't get the chance. Margo suddenly appeared, seemingly out of thin air. Margo's petiteness coupled with her brown dress, the same color as the hotel's exterior, had made Margo barely noticeable. In Eve's peripheral vision, Margo had been camouflaged against the backdrop of the hotel. Margo grabbed her husband's arm. "I need to speak to you," she said roughly.

Eve took the hint and walked away as she again

wondered why Margo Wells was even at this event. It wasn't because she enjoyed her husband's company. But, who knew? Codependence has many faces, Eve told herself. She again felt overwhelmed by the personalities around her and debated whether she should take a page out of Naiya's book and take a break before tackling the evening portion of the day. It didn't take her long to decide. The thought of a little alone time won her over. She decided that everyone could do without her presence for a short while.

When she entered the lobby, she was amazed to see that Loretta and Roxie had already moved all the folding chairs and arranged the lobby couches and chairs back into its cozy sitting room layout. Henry, Sheila, and Kelly were already taking advantage of it, relaxing on the couches and chatting. On her way through the lobby to her manager's suite, Eve grabbed one of the conference itineraries that were sitting on a table. She went into her small apartment and was happy to see that Wes had deposited Sunset and Midas in her room. They were both exhausted from their day of gallivanting. Midas was sprawled out on Sunset's bed and Sunset was curled up on one side of the love seat. Both dogs were too tired to bother to get up to greet her but at least they were polite enough to open their eyes halfway and give her entrance a little musical accompaniment. Their percussion tails slowly and steadily beat on their drum beds to let her know they were happy to see her. She joined Sunset on the loveseat, put her feet up on her tiny coffee table, and flipped through the pages of the conference schedule.

Tomorrow's schedule mimicked today's, with the same speakers and varied subjects. Each lecture had the presenter's name and the subject written. Most of the classes sounded very technical. Things like, Gabriel Spurlock: Management of Neuropathic pain, and Olive Hudson: Effect of altrenogest on endogenous progesterone during early pregnancy in recipient mares.

But she was interested in sitting in on Lorenzo's talk on the last day about "Thinking Like a Horse." She thought she might understand that one. She then noticed that the last talk of the conference had Dr. Arthur Wells's name written in it but no subject. She wondered if it was a typo. It was set as an hour-long talk, so it couldn't be a simple "goodbye and thank you."

At about 4:30, Eve received a text from Wes saying he had left Blaze in the stable a little while ago for Naiya and was now out at the tumbleweed pen. The ping on her phone had popped her eyes open, which alerted her to the fact that they had been closed. She decided to make herself a cup of coffee to get her through the rest of the day. The days were already so much longer than in the winter. She used to always hate the short days of winter but now she was missing them. When it got dark at 5:30 you could justify going to bed really early. Which, it occurred to her was a new thing she had started to enjoy. She felt the slow but steady pull into elderliness, and it didn't sound so bad, not bad at all. But, at least, for this evening she would fight it off with caffeine.

At 5:00, Eve was ready to make her way out to the stables. The boys were still asleep, which was good. She didn't want to take them out to the stables for Naiya's first exam of Blaze, and this way she didn't have to endure an excruciating puppy-eyes whimpering-filled guilt trip. She left as quietly as possible to not wake them. As usual (if unaccompanied by canine companions) she decided to walk through the lobby rather than exiting out the side door. It was her habit to always walk through the lobby so that she could check in and make an appearance in case someone needed her for something. After closing the door behind her, she paused to make sure she hadn't forgotten her keys and her phone. While she stood there checking her pockets for a moment, she listened to the hushed gossipy conversation between Henry, Sheila, and Kelly who were still sitting on the lobby couches.

"Oh, sure, I've heard of him," said Henry. "Hasn't everyone in the greater Phoenix area?"

"Every woman has, I know that," said Kelly with a laugh.

"Every married woman," added Sheila.

"And you don't need to hear about him, you can just smell him!" said Henry.

Kelly laughed. "His cologne is rather strong, isn't it?"

"It's invasive!" Henry said. "It lingers. You can smell where he was five minutes ago."

"I like it," said Sheila.

Kelly laughed again, even louder. "You would!"

Eve deduced that they were talking about Lorenzo. She had also noticed the strength of his cologne. Henry was right, Lorenzo wore too much of it. But luckily, it was a nice smell that had notes of sandalwood and clove. Eve found it to be quite an alluring scent and didn't mind at all that it lingered.

"But he's very good at what he does," said Henry.

"You mean who he does," said Sheila.

Kelly laughed even louder, verging on cackling as she said, "and he does a lot."

"I meant that he's a good horse trainer!" Henry said joining in the laughter.

"Yes, I heard he's good at that too," said Sheila.

Eve turned and, to pretend that she hadn't been listening, she said the first thing that came to her mind, "Hi! I was just looking at the conference schedule. Do any of you know what the last presentation is about? I noticed it didn't have a subject."

"Oh, I've heard it's a secret," Henry said. "I believe Dr. Wells asked for it to remain a mystery so he could have a big reveal."

"A big reveal? Of what?"

"It's a secret," Sheila reminded her as she winked.

"It's probably something very medical and scientific," said Kelly. "It might be interesting to us, but I doubt it will be to you."

"You're probably right!" Eve laughed. "I could barely read some of the titles to the talks. Just a reminder, dinner service starts at six," she said as she walked away.

After exiting the back door, Eve remembered that she never texted Wes back. She continued walking as she texted him a quick "thanks." It only took a second of texting while walking to cause an accident. As she hit the send button on her phone, she simultaneously ran into a wall of a body and stepped on a foot in a cowboy boot.

"Ow," said the owner of the body and the abused foot.

"Oh!" Eve exclaimed with her hand to her chest. "Burt. You scared me. Where did you come from?"

"Scared of little old me?" Burt said with an easy smile.

Eve looked up at the man who could not be described as little or old. Strapping is the word that came to mind. "Are you okay?" she asked, looking down at his foot.

"Yes, I'm fine."

"What are you up to?" Eve said, trying not to telegraph her thoughts that Naiya had horrible taste in nemeses. Burt's eyes were too kind to play the part of an evil opponent.

"I've been looking around the property. I'm impressed. I wanted to tell you how happy I am that you restored this place. I used to drive by it all the time and think what a great place this could be. You've really made it into one. Good on you."

*It's official, worst nemesis ever!* Eve laughed to herself before replying with, "Thank you so much. I really appreciate that. It's been a lot of work but all worth it."

"You inherited the place, right? From family?"

"In a roundabout way. I inherited it from family but it wasn't my family that had owned it originally. But my great aunt who gave it to me used to spend a lot of time here. She really loved this property. I couldn't just sell it or let it fall into ruins. Being here makes me feel eternally connected to her. And now I can't imagine living anywhere else."

"I know exactly what you mean. Hey, are you possibly heading out to see your new horse?"

"Why yes, I am. I'm meeting Naiya out there. She's giving him an introductory examination."

"Do you mind if I join you? I must admit, I'm fascinated by his peculiarity. I think we all are."

"Yes, it certainly seemed that way."

He laughed. "That's our job. We like fixing problems."

"Sure, come on," Eve said without thinking. They were walking along the path before Eve realized that Naiya might not appreciate the uninvited guest. In fact, she was sure Naiya wouldn't like having her professional rival stand over her watching as she worked. Eve suddenly regretted the invitation. She should be on her friend's side. Perhaps there was something to Naiya's distrust of Dr. Burt. She suddenly felt she had an obligation to vet him. "So, Burt, what took you away from Juniper County and what made you come back?"

"Oh, um," he began slowly, "it's just one of those 'the grass is always greener' things."

*Vague*, Eve thought. *But suspicious? Untrustworthy?*

But before she could press him for more information, she saw Naiya walking toward them on the path from the stables. Eve's first thought was that Naiya had seen them coming and was putting a stop to Burt's inclusion. But that thought only lasted a moment. She could tell that wasn't Naiya's angry march. Eve was confused. Confusion quickly turned to concern as Naiya came closer. The look on Naiya's face scared Eve. Something was wrong, terribly wrong.

## Chapter Five

Naiya's face was contorted into a look of horror as she continued to walk toward Eve and Burt. She tripped on an uneven part of the path. As she stumbled and caught herself, she let out the sob that she had obviously been holding in. Burt rushed to Naiya's side and put his arm around her to steady her stance.

"What is it?" Eve asked her.

Naiya was incapable of speech as further sobs erupted. She used one hand to cover her face and the other to point at the stables.

Eve's first thought was of Wes. The stables were his domain. But it couldn't be anything wrong with Wes, he was out at the tumbleweed pen. The tumbleweed pen with the woodchipper. Eve had the most terrible thought before reminding herself that Naiya was pointing in the opposite direction. The stables, there was something wrong at the stables. Eve left Burt comforting Naiya as her feet caught up to her racing mind and she ran all the way there.

After she entered the building, it took Eve a minute to drink in the scene. No Blaze. A broken and splintered stable door. And in the stable itself, a crushed tumbleweed, pieces of it everywhere, including on… Eve closed her eyes for a brief second, hoping in vain that when she opened them again she wouldn't see it— him, that she wouldn't see him. But when she opened her eyes, he was still there. She could barely see his face. His arms were covering most of it, evidence of a futile attempt to protect himself. But she was sure it was him: a bloodied, stomped on, and unmoving Art Wells.

Eve felt sick. This was all her fault. Blaze had done this. She brought him here. Eve gave herself only a few moments to let the panic and guilt take over. Then she forced away the unbearable feelings so she could think of what to do. Within a minute she had a plan. She first verified that Art did not have a pulse. Then she called Wes. After that, she asked Burt to take sobbing Naiya into the privacy of the laundry room building to calm down. Fifteen minutes later, Eve called the sheriff.

While waiting for the sheriff and ambulance to arrive, she made her way to the laundry building on the kitchen side of the hotel. When she walked in, she was happy to see that Naiya was a little more composed. Eve asked Naiya and Burt to follow her into the hotel so they could give everyone the dreadful news. They entered through the kitchen and found Esperanza and Ramon. She motioned for them to follow her. Everyone needed to know what had happened. Eve led the march into the lobby, almost hitting Colin and Reid with the swinging door. Colin and Reid both had their phones in their hands. Colin looked incredibly happy. Eve's heart sank as she looked at the smile on Colin's face, sadly thinking that her news would soon be extinguishing all smiles, joy, and laughter.

Esperanza and Ramon helped gather Loretta, Roxie, and all of the guests together quickly. Eve wanted to break the news before the law and medical vehicles arrived to the property. After everyone was gathered, most of them staring worriedly at Naiya's tear-stained face, Eve explained the situation as best and as calmly as she could.

"No!" exclaimed Olive as she clasped her hand to her mouth only to immediately remove it to add, "Poor Art!"

A brief silence overtook the room. Eve looked around at the faces that all displayed versions of shock and confusion. All except Margo's. Margo simply appeared pensive.

"Poor Blaze," Colin said, his smile a thing of the past. "And Art, of course."

"I don't understand," said Gabriel. "A tumbleweed blew into the stables?"

"I don't understand, either," said Henry. "Why was Art out there?"

Margo shook off her thoughtfulness and replaced it with a scowl. "He wanted to see that stupid horse," she said with annoyance. "He probably thought he could hug the horse's problem out of him."

Eve was sickened by Margo's reaction at hearing about the death of her husband.

"A tumbleweed couldn't have blown into the stables, could it?" asked Sheila.

"It had to," said Lorenzo. "It was obviously some horribly unlikely sequence of events."

"Unless... maybe Art brought it in with him?" Reid suggested. "Maybe he had reconsidered the immersion therapy technique."

"No. I don't think so," said Olive.

"Maybe," said Burt.

"No," repeated Olive. "He wouldn't do that. He wouldn't suddenly go against everything he believed and try to scare the horse straight. Don't be stupid." Olive looked apologetically at Burt. "Sorry," she said as a single tear escaped from her eye.

Naiya's body shuddered with another sob and Burt put his arm around her again. "You're fine," Burt kindly said to Olive. "And you're right. He wouldn't do that."

"It had to be an accident," said Kelly. "Just a freak

accident."

"Yes," Reid said as he put his hand on Kelly's shoulder in a comforting fashion. "I'm sure it is."

Eve noticed Sheila's brief look of jealousy before she joined in as everyone started nodding their heads in agreement that the event was a sad, tragic accident.

Eve desperately wanted to think that Art's death was an accident, but she couldn't. The introduction of a tumbleweed in the stables could not have been a chance occurrence. The tumbleweed did not blow into the stables building and it certainly didn't jump into the stable itself. The stable door had been locked, the wood had splintered around it, finally letting a hysterical Blaze free. Art had entered the stable and locked the door to examine Blaze. He could not have been able to do that if he was for some reason holding a tumbleweed. No. Art was in there with Blaze when a tumbleweed was introduced to the scene, meaning someone had to have brought it in and placed it in the enclosed space with the horse and the veterinarian. Of course, whether it was some sick joke or the intention was murder, Eve did not know.

Eve tried to fight off another wave of crushing guilt. Yes, someone else did this repulsive act, but Eve gave them the idea. She told the whole room about Blaze's problem. She tried to tell herself that it wasn't her fault that someone took that information and turned it into a murderous opportunity. But she couldn't help wonder if Art would be alive right now if she just would have kept her mouth shut. Would Art not be crushed and littered with tumbleweed thorns? As her thoughts bombarded her, the feelings of guilt were outweighed by the absurdity of a death caused by a tumbleweed.

She even knew what tumbleweed had been used: the one Colin had wrangled earlier. When Eve went to get Naiya and Burt from the laundry room, she saw that the interim pen was empty, the tumbleweed was gone. Before Wes had left, she asked him if he had brought it to the big pen. He said no. Someone took that tumbleweed and used it to kill Art. She looked around the room to see if she could see guilt on anyone's face but no one looked guilty. Sad, forlorn, confused, but not guilty. Except Margo. Margo's expression of calculated musing had returned.

"I need to see him," Olive said suddenly and rushed out of the room towards the back door.

Eve was amazed at how fast Olive's short legs propelled her away from the group. Olive was gone before Eve could tell her no. "She can't do that," Eve said pathetically as she stood with the others.

"Why not?" asked Jessica. "You're not a doctor. Olive is. I know she's a vet, not an M.D. but still, she's better than you. No offence, but I'd feel better if she gave us the definitive word on the subject of Art's status."

Just as everyone had nodded in agreement that Art's death was an accident, they now nodded in agreement that Eve was not fit to make the call about Art's prognosis. Eve felt stupid and embarrassed and didn't know what to say. She looked toward Naiya for support but found none. Naiya was in another world, still overcome with the upsetting sight she had just witnessed. She had gone from uncontrollably sobbing to a state of zombie-like shock. Burt still stood next to her with his arm around her shoulder. Eve was fairly certain that he alone was keeping Naiya upright.

Eve wasn't sure what to do but felt she needed to do something. She decided to follow Olive out to the stables. She didn't want to see the scene again, but she also wanted to make sure that nothing was disturbed. As she walked along the path, she felt a gust of cold wind and saw a white flutter out of the corner of her eyes. She always thought spring was such a strange time of year in the high elevation desert of northern Arizona. It was as if winter and summer were violently fighting over domination. There was always a time in spring when the white flutter could either be the white petals of the already dying flowers on the property's ornamental trees or it could be snow. She turned her face into the wind and when the cold flakes stung her face, she realized that this time it was snow. Winter had taken the lead in the battle.

When she arrived at the stables, she found a motionless Olive standing over Art's body. "You were right. He's gone. How sad. He was such a good man."

"Did you know him? Know him well?"

"Of course. We were business partners."

"Oh," said Eve. "I didn't know that."

"Yes, we've ran our practice together for, oh, I think it's about eight years now."

"Oh," Eve said again. She was interested to learn that Olive was close with Art but her mind was elsewhere. Eve was simultaneously anxiously awaiting and dreading the arrival of the sheriff. What was she going to say to him? What was he going to do?

"We became good friends during that time as well," said Olive, interrupting Eve's thoughts. "I don't know what I'm going to do without him."

"I'm so sorry for your loss," Eve said with feeling, as she discarded her selfish thoughts and focused on Olive. "I had no idea you two were so close. It's such a tragedy."

Olive didn't say anything. Her intelligent gray-blue eyes darted around the room from Art to the pieces of tumbleweed to the broken stable door and beyond. As Eve watched Olive she felt a creeping desperation to move the conversation to a different location. Eve was about to suggest it when Olive surprised her.

"You know this is murder, right?" Olive said as she looked at Art's body.

After Eve caught her breath, she replied, "Yes. I came to the same conclusion."

Olive once again surprised Eve by saying, "I'm going to find out who did it."

## Chapter Six

Olive insisted on staying with Art until the sheriff arrived and Eve couldn't let Olive remain alone. Luckily, it wasn't too long before their sad, silent vigil ended. Sheriff Strider and Deputy Navarro arrived and instructed Olive and Eve to wait back at the hotel. Eve was happy to leave.

When Eve and Olive returned to the hotel they found the group of hotel guests gathered where they had left them in the lobby, all anxiously awaiting further news of the tragedy. Olive immediately voiced her opinion that, "Art was murdered," while giving the entire group a blanket accusatory stare down.

"No!" Colin exclaimed.

Olive explained why she believed it was murder, which coincided with Eve's deductions. As Olive's statement sunk in, everyone's expressions slowly turned to horror or disbelief.

"Maybe it was a prank gone wrong," suggested Lorenzo.

"Even if it was a prank that went horribly wrong and ended in murder, that's still murder," offered Henry.

"Manslaughter," said Jessica. "That's what they call it. Isn't it?"

"But just because it wasn't premeditated doesn't mean it's not still murder," said Olive.

"And maybe it was," said Sheila. "Maybe it was premeditated." She looked around the room with a wide-eyed fear at her fellow hotel guests.

"I'm sure it wasn't," Reid said reassuringly to Sheila as he patted her on the shoulder.

His affection took immediate effect. Sheila calmed and even smiled at Reid as she said, "I'm sure you're right."

The rest of the group could not be as easily placated as Sheila. Everyone had an opinion about Olive's hypothesis. Eve walked away in a daze leaving Olive to deal with the onslaught of questions and criticisms being hurled at her. Eve had other things on her mind as she walked back into the dining room and stared out the floor to ceiling windows towards the stables. She nervously wondered what would happen next. Her thoughts were as scattered as the tiny snowflakes swirling in the wind. Her anxiety started enveloping her once again. She thought that if she were to ever take up the bad habit of biting her fingernails, now might be the time. It must be comforting in some weird way, she thought. She almost stuck her finger into her mouth to try it when she remembered the filth that fingers held. When was the last time she even washed her hands? What had she touched since she had last washed her hands? When she realized one of the things had been the wrist of a murdered man's corpse, her disgust made her body shake.

It seemed like forever before Art's body was taken away. And yet, that forever seemed too soon as Eve watched the sheriff and the deputy walk towards the hotel. She only slightly registered that the wind had died down and the snowflakes had become bigger and fluffier.

Eve had already suspended dinner service, so she offered the empty dining room to Deputy Navarro to take statements from the hotel guests.

As the three who had been witness to the aftermath of Art's tragedy, Naiya, Olive, and Eve were selected to be interviewed by the sheriff. Eve let the sheriff use her office to first interview Naiya and then Olive. When it was finally Eve's turn, she was nervous. Very nervous. Not filthy nail biting nervous, but very very nervous.

She first told him how she had come upon Naiya and then went to the stables. She explained what she had seen. She hoped, although she knew it was in vain, that he would be satisfied with the information she presented him and move on to solving Art's murder. But instead, he asked the question she was dreading.

"Where's the horse?"

Her heart was beating so loudly, she was sure that the sheriff could hear it. "He's not here."

"Where is he?"

"I don't know."

Sheriff Strider silently looked without expression at Eve for so long it made her feel ill. He finally said, "You know that in this situation, I need to bring him in."

"I know. But…" Eve was fighting to stay emotionless. "This isn't his fault. Someone used him to commit murder. Someone abused this animal. You can't blame him. You can't put him down. It's not fair. He's just an innocent animal. This is the work of a calculating human. You can't blame Blaze. You can't take him and…"

"But I can't take him in if he's not here."

"He's not here."

"And you don't know where he is."

"I do not." Eve held her breath waiting for more questions about Blaze. Relief washed over her when the sheriff changed subjects.

"Dr. Hudson is sure that this is murder. You obviously agree."

"Yes."

"What is it about this property?" He sighed and gave

her a friendly look that made Eve relax even more.

"I don't know." She also sighed. "I've wondered about that myself. My theory is that the isolated location of the hotel makes people think that the rules of the real world don't apply here. Survival of the meanest. Every gunslinger for himself. Wild West Syndrome, patent pending."

The sheriff fought off a smile. "Tell me your theory."

By the time she had told him all her thoughts on the subject of Art's tragic demise, Deputy Navarro knocked at the door to hand his notes to the sheriff.

"It's starting to snow harder," said the serious young deputy with the angular facial features of a brooding silent film star.

"You head back to the station while you can," said the sheriff. "I'll stay here."

"Yes, sir," said the deputy and left.

The sheriff flipped through the notes Deputy Navarro had handed him. "It looks like during the window of opportunity, we only have three people who alibi out: Henry Bayless, Kelly Cheesborough, and Sheila Kamnitz. They were apparently in the lobby talking to each other between the time Art was last seen after the conference ended at around 4:00 and when he was found at 5:00."

"That's correct," said Eve. "Or at least, they were there when I went into my suite at about 4:15 and they were still there when I left to go to the stables at 5:oo."

"Not only are they each other's alibis, but in the statements of others they also mention seeing the three of them sitting in the lobby throughout the timeframe. We can eliminate them from our list of suspects."

"That's good."

"But they're the only ones. Looks like everyone else was alone for the majority of the hour. You know, I really wish you would have listened to me a long time ago—"

"And installed security cameras," she finished for him. "I know. Trust me. I know. In fact, look." She moved some binders that had been sitting on top of a cardboard box in the corner. The top of the box read: indoor/outdoor security camera system. "Ramon was going to install the system as soon as the conference was over."

"That figures," he said with a disappointed head shake. "But thank you for getting them."

Eve was secretly happy that they hadn't installed the security cameras yet. Yes, being able to see who had walked out to the stables would have been nice, but they would have also filmed something that Eve needed to keep from the sheriff. "So, who does that leave us with as suspects?" she asked.

"Ms. Cordova and Dr. Nadar..."

Eve rolled her eyes. "It wasn't me or Naiya."

"There's your staff," said the sheriff.

"Those are fightin' words," she responded with only a hint of humor.

"Okay, okay," he said. "Onsite during the incident with no alibi are... Dr. Wells's wife Margo Wells, horse trainer Lorenzo Dominguez, and veterinarian Doctors Hudson, Tolliver, McCullough, Denmon, Bullock, and Spurlock."

"You don't think Olive Hudson had anything to do with it, do you? She's the one who called it out as murder. She wants to find who did this."

"Murderers don't adhere to the social conventions that we expect. It's a possibility she's just trying to throw you off her scent. Plus, she was partners with the deceased. Now the business might be hers alone, right? It might be motive." He grunted with exasperation. "I hate cases like this."

"Like what?"

"I usually rely on the stupidity of criminals to catch them. This is a group of intelligent respected veterinarians. Cunning suspects change the game completely."

"My money's on the wife. That lady is as cold as they come."

"Ok, I'll speak with her first. Will you send her in, please?"

"Sure," Eve said and stood.

"Also, while you're out there, find out if anyone else was connected to Arthur Wells."

"Try to stop me," she said with a wink before shutting the door behind her.

Eve found Margo sitting in the dining room with Reid, Lorenzo, and Gabriel. People weren't interested in eating, but they were interested in drinking. Loretta had taken the bartender post. Before Eve could make her way to Margo, Loretta waved her over to the bar.

"Hey," Loretta said quietly, "I hope you don't mind but I got the dogs out of your suite and gave 'em to Naiya. She's real sad and wanted some pet love."

"No problem, thanks. Is she okay? Do you think I should check on her?"

"She's good. Dr. Burt's with her."

"Oh. Okay."

Loretta walked off and Eve stood wondering if she should still check in on Naiya.

Behind her, Eve heard Reid say, "It's snowing. How are my allergies not subsiding? My nose must be training for a marathon because it just keeps running and running." Eve turned just in time to see him, once again, automatically wipe his nose on the sleeve of his sweater. "Ow," he said as he jerked his arm away. He looked slightly embarrassed as he said, "My nose is getting raw."

"That's what you get for wiping your nose on your clothing," Margo said nastily, this time offering an eyeroll instead of a tissue.

"I thought cashmere was supposed to be soft," said Gabriel. "I'd think it would make the ideal high-end tissue. They should make cashmere handkerchiefs. Who knows, maybe they do. If I ever become afflicted with allergies, perhaps I'll look into it."

"Have you ever noticed that rich people things all start with 'c'?" Lorenzo said. "Cashmere, champagne, caviar…"

"What?" barked Margo. "That's the stupidest thing I've ever heard. Especially from a man wearing a fortune on his feet. I know how much those boots cost."

"I'm sorry," said Lorenzo sheepishly. "I'm just trying to distract myself from thinking about the appalling accident."

"But I suppose you could add 'cowboy boots' to your list of rich people things," Margo continued nastily. "Those are the most expensive brand of boots available. How did you afford those?"

"They were a gift," Lorenzo said with less of an apologetic tone.

"She must be some rich lady," said Margo with a sneer.

"Yes," Lorenzo said with absolutely no apology left in his tone. "She's quite wealthy. So wealthy, in fact, that she can afford the exact brand-new limited-edition purse that you're carrying. How did you afford that?"

"I'm a widow now," Margo said with her chin jutted out. "Have some respect or shut up."

"Margo!" Eve said loudly, more loudly than she had intended, but she didn't regret it. "The sheriff wants to speak with 'the widow.' Now. In my office." Eve wanted Margo to know that she was not the one in charge and that her viciousness in the wake of her kind husband's death was not welcome.

Margo had the decency to follow Eve without another word. As Eve led the widow to the office, she reminded herself that people grieve in different ways. To Eve it appeared that Margo was not grieving at all, but angrily lashing out might be Margo's coping mechanism in the face of such a devasting loss. Eve doubted it but she hated thinking that people were capable of such callousness.

She always hoped there was kindness hiding somewhere behind cruelty. As she opened the door to the office and looked at Sheriff Strider, she realized he had to have a much greater resolve than she. Faced with the challenges of his job every single day, it was practically a miracle that he kept as sunny of a disposition as he did. Eve realized that retaining hope in humanity was one of his greatest attributes and one of the things she liked most about him.

After delivering Margo to the sheriff, she followed Colin as he joined the group in the dining room. Although Eve did have every intention of helping the sheriff, and Olive, find Art Wells's murderer, she had another pressing concern weighing heavily on her. She looked around the room at Colin, Reid, Lorenzo, and Gabriel. Perhaps it was a conflict of interest, but she didn't know what else to do. She needed help.

In the end, it didn't take as long as she thought it would and it didn't work out how she had expected, but she was still satisfied with the end result. By the time the sheriff had finished his interview with Margo, everything had been arranged. Eve was so happy, perhaps too happy. Perhaps she shouldn't have been hugging one of the murder suspects. She certainly wished she hadn't been hugging the famous and charming Dr. Reid Tolliver when Margo and Sheriff Strider walked into the room.

## Chapter Seven

Eve abruptly ended the hug, pushing Reid away from her too quickly to not be on the side of rude. She kept her eyes on the sheriff to see his reaction, but his face betrayed nothing. His calm professional demeanor remained intact as he deposited Margo in the dining room with the others and asked Reid to follow him to the office. Eve could not tell if it had been the sheriff's premeditated intention to question Reid next or if it was an impulsive decision.

As the sheriff and Reid walked away, Eve once again looked around the room, this time at her remaining confidants: Colin, Gabriel, and Lorenzo. Not only had she confided in Reid, but these three other men were now privy to her secret. They had promised to keep quiet about it, but would they? Eve was in a strange predicament having to trust the very people she was also having to suspect of murder.

Eve's head jerked to the side when she realized someone was standing next to her. It was Margo. Margo was also staring at the three men in the dining room with a similar look of contemplation. Eve shared a secret with these men and now she was sharing a facial expression with Margo? She was confused. What could Margo be wondering? She certainly did not have the same dilemma as Eve.

But Eve's interest in Margo was only momentary. As Eve watched Colin and Lorenzo walk out the back door into the snowfall, her thoughts reverted back to her questionable judgment in trusting these men.

Margo sat with Gabriel and shot Eve a look as if she was not welcome. Eve didn't mind. She was suddenly overwhelmed with the need to physically distance herself from these strangers and be with someone she actually trusted. She went out to the lobby to see if she could find Naiya. As she entered, she saw the front door close. She hurried to the other side of the room and went out to the cold porch but found only Burt.

"It's really coming down," Burt said looking at the cascade of snowflakes that had dusted the world white around them.

"Have you seen Naiya?" Eve asked.

"She's in her room lying down. She was really upset. She needed some rest and alone time."

"Oh." Eve was disappointed. She needed some friend time.

"The sheriff took Reid into your office to interview him?" Burt asked.

"Yes, but I don't know why, other than—," she stopped herself. Burt didn't need to know about the hug, or why it happened, or why the sheriff may have had an adverse reaction to seeing it. "Never mind." She wrapped her arms around herself since she had walked out without a jacket. "I'm sure there's no connection between him and Art."

Burt raised an eyebrow as he looked at her and said, "Yes, there is."

"There is?"

"Sure. They're old friends. They used to be partners a long time ago."

"They did? How do you know this? Oh wait, you know Reid somehow, right?"

"No."

"I thought you were the one who got him to speak at the conference."

"No. That was Art."

"What?" she asked, feeling increasingly stupid. She thought she had started her inquiries at square one but now realized she had some catching up to do. She felt like she was at square negative five.

"I know Art," Burt said. "I don't know Reid. At least, I didn't before I met him here. I met Art a few years ago, we hit it off and became friends. When I saw he was speaking at a conference right here in Juniper County, I couldn't believe it. That's why I wanted to come to the conference, to see Art. Then Naiya told me she was down a speaker and was thinking about canceling the conference, so I called up Art and asked him if he knew anybody that could fill in. To my surprise he ended up securing Reid."

Eve's first thought was that if Art and Reid had been partners then Margo and Reid had known each other for a long time. It made much more sense to Eve that Margo felt so comfortable talking to Reid in such a condescending way. "Oh. So, Reid and Margo know each other as well?" she asked for confirmation.

"I suppose so. Art and Margo have been married a long time."

"And you have a connection to Art also," Eve said, stating the obvious as she calculated how much more complicated the situation was becoming.

"It's a sad day for a lot of us. Art was a truly good man and veterinarian. I'm having a hard time with this…" Burt paused before spitting out the word, "accident."

"Do you not think it was an accident?"

"I don't know."

"Do you agree with Olive? Do you think it was

murder?"

To Eve's surprise, Burt laughed. "Murder? Someone murder kind and wonderful Art Wells? No. Of course not. Everyone loved him. Every person and every animal that ever met him loved him."

"Even his wife?" Eve asked skeptically.

"She did at some point. And I think when it comes to Margo, that's really saying something."

"So, what do you think happened?"

"I don't know, but I can't stop thinking about the debate about your horse. Gabriel and Art really butt heads. What if Gabriel was trying to prove his theory to Art and things took a turn. I don't know. It was obviously some sort of horrifying miscalculation, but someone is to blame and it isn't the horse and it certainly isn't Art. It's someone here."

Eve's body shuddered with the chill of the thought. Then she realized that it probably wasn't just the thought, it was also freezing outside. She excused herself and returned to the warmth of the lobby.

Her desire for the comfort of a friend was forgotten. The cold had energized her body and the realization of her ignorance of Art's relationships had motivated her mind. She needed to learn more about how Art was connected to each of her hotel guests. Eve noticed that Margo was sitting by herself in the lobby. Now that she knew Margo knew Reid, Eve thought she'd take advantage of Reid's absence and ask her about him.

Eve didn't know how to ease into the conversation, so she didn't. She plopped down on a chair near Margo and asked, "Do you think Reid did it?"

Margo looked at her but said nothing as she regarded the abrupt question. After a few beats she began to say something, then stopped, returning to her silent stare.

Eve thought maybe she didn't understand the question, so she clarified. "Do you think Reid caused the tumbleweed situation that killed Art?

With eyebrows drawn together, Margo finally said, "Why would you ask me that?" in her habitually annoyed tone.

"Just wondering. Art and Reid were partners a long time ago, right?"

"Correct."

"There must be history there. Why did they dissolve their partnership? Did something bad happen?"

"Yes, in fact, it did."

"What?"

"Why?"

"Because I'm interested in him," said Eve weakly.

"It's none of your business."

Eve wracked her brain thinking of a way to get Margo to talk to her. "Come on," Eve said conspiratorially. "Reid is famous and so interesting. And you are friends with him. Aren't you?"

Margo didn't answer.

"Oh," said Eve. "I'm sorry. Maybe you aren't as close as I thought you were. I guess that makes sense. I mean, he's so wealthy. I'm sure he runs with a different crowd."

Eve's plan worked. Margo was quick to claim membership to the club of the rich and famous. "Don't be stupid," she said. "Of course, I know him well. I've known him for many years. I know all sorts of things about Reid."

"So, what happened with his and Art's partnership?" Eve said, adopting the persona of an eager gossip.

"Little Jessie Laberge. She's the bad thing that happened. It's her fault. She ended their partnership."

"And who is that?" Eve prodded.

"A snotty little rich teenager who thought her horse was her best friend."

"What happened?"

"Her horse died. She blamed Art and Reid. Art felt guilty, Reid didn't. They fought and then fought some more and then eventually went their separate ways. It's too bad really. If Art stayed with Reid, if they could have come to some sort of agreement, Art could have been making all that money with Reid. But no, he had to be a goody two shoes, as always. For the last fifteen years or so, he could have been making real money, but no. His bleeding-heart guilt and ethics have been the bane of my existence."

Margo made Eve sick. Her husband had just died and here she was still complaining that he hadn't made enough money for her. Eve swallowed her disgust, forced a neutral expression, and kept a conversational tone as she asked, "But Art and Reid remained friends?"

"No," Margo said as her mind and eyes drifted elsewhere.

As Margo stared across the room overtaken by her thoughts, Colin walked into the room and flashed Eve an "A-OK" hand signal. Eve nodded in understanding but wanted to finish her conversation with Margo. "No?" she said as a prompt.

"Hmmm?" Margo looked back towards Eve. "Oh. Oh, yes. Art and Reid."

"They didn't remain friends," Eve said to remind her of the conversation.

"No. Art and Reid didn't speak for years. They only reconnected recently. Art always saw the best in people. Sometimes, even when it wasn't there."

"Excuse me," said Colin, who had stopped and turned before he climbed the stairs. He walked over to Margo and Eve and said, "Reid Tolliver is a saint."

Margo rolled her eyes. To Eve, she said, "Another one from the bleeding-heart brigade." Then, to Colin, she said, "Saints don't exist." Then to no one in particular she said, "I need to call my attorney." Margo stood and went upstairs to her suite.

"Reid is a good man," Colin said to Eve. "You know he is. He just helped you out. And shortly before that, he helped me out— big time."

"What did he do for you?"

Colin sat down, leaned in, and whispered, "He donated to my horse sanctuary. A lot. He donated a lot. I thought I would ask for a large amount, hoping that he would feel guilty and give me just a fraction of that, but he gave me the whole amount! I still can't believe it. I was struggling to keep my sanctuary open and now I can relax. It's nothing short of a miracle. And that's why I'm sticking to my assertion that Reid is a saint." Colin paused as the happy look on his face faded. "But, I suppose, I should be thanking Art. Art suggested I ask Reid for the donation. Maybe Art put in a good word for me."

"Maybe Reid was feeling philanthropic after finding out about the death of his friend," suggested Eve.

"No. It was right before you told us about Art. It was just out of the goodness of his heart. But, like I said, I should be giving Art some credit. He probably greased the wheels. Art was like that. He really believed in what I was doing. In fact, Art said that he would—" Colin stopped mid-sentence and turned white as a ghost.

"What is it?"

"I… I just remembered something."

"What?"

"I don't… I can't… I'm not sure…" Then, unintentionally parroting Margo, Colin said, "I need to call my attorney."

As Eve watched Colin walk away, she wondered why everyone suddenly needed legal help.

## Chapter Eight

After Colin had left Eve alone in the lobby, she began mentally cataloguing what she had learned about her guests thus far. But it wasn't long before her quiet contemplation was interrupted. First by the chatty group of Sheila, Kelly, and Henry who came and sat across the coffee table from her, and then by Jessica who came in and asked if anyone would like to play chess. Henry accepted her invitation and followed her to the chess table against the wall.

Then the office door opened. As soon as Reid came out and closed the door behind him, he made immediate eye contact with Eve and gravitated towards her like he was caught in a powerful tractor beam. Reid didn't pay attention to anyone else in the room, not Sheila who was looking at him with affection, nor Jessica who was giving him the evil eye. Eve wasn't sure if it was because of his confidence, his celebrity status, or the fact that he had helped her, but she couldn't deny that she was flattered to be the recipient of the man's attention. She flashed him a smile and stood to greet him but abandoned that plan as soon as she saw Naiya open the door to her lobby level suite wiping her nose with a tissue.

Eve immediately walked over to Naiya and gave her a quick hug. "Are you okay?"

"Yes. No. I don't know."

"I thought you were going to rest for awhile," Eve said with feeling as she looked at her friend's puffy eyes and red nose.

"I tried, but Emily called to see how the conference was going. She was not happy with my answer."

"Sorry," Eve said, not knowing what else could be said.

Naiya looked around the room at the others and silently waved as an indication for Eve to follow her back into her suite. As soon as Eve walked into the room, she was bombarded with dog love. Sunset and Midas had not been briefed on the gravitas of the situation. Their joy had not been dampened by the sad news about Art. Eve was happy Naiya had them during this difficult time. There really was no better therapy than being showered with dog love. Eve was on her knees letting the wiggly, tail wagging, hairy, slobbery love wash over her as Naiya said, "I asked Emily why she decided to hold this conference in northern Arizona."

Eve stood and wiped the hairy and slobbery part of the dog love off of her. "Oh yeah? What did she say?"

"Emily was organizing it around Art because there was an announcement that he wanted to make publicly, I guess. He was going to use the conference to unveil something and he specifically asked that the conference be held in northern Arizona."

"But why?"

"She didn't know. She liked and trusted Art, so she just did what he asked. Emily is really upset." Naiya's shoulders sagged.

Eve gave Naiya another quick hug and another, "Sorry." Then she remembered something she had been wanting to ask Naiya. "Hey, when you went out to see

Blaze, did you see Burt walking around? Maybe coming from the stables?"

"What?!" Naiya exclaimed defensively. "No! Don't you think that I would have told you that?"

"I don't know," said Eve. "You were upset, in shock. You may have forgotten or it didn't register as important at the time."

"No, I didn't see him. I didn't see anyone."

"Ok. I just thought I should ask. I mean, he was outside and appeared out of nowhere. Thinking back on it, I can't help but wonder if that was strange. I just want to find out what happened," she added with frustration. "We have to find out what happened to Art."

In the somber silence that followed, it was easy to hear the commotion coming from the lobby on the other side of the closed door. Naiya and Eve went into the lobby, leaving Sunset and Midas in the room even though the two dogs were equally interested in investigating the source of the loud, enraged voice.

Margo's heels angrily clicked and clacked on the stairs as she marched down while yelling, "Where is he? Where is that conniving thief?" When Margo reached the bottom of the stairs she stood with her hands on her hips, whipping her head around, back and forth as she surveyed the room.

"Who?" Eve asked as Gabriel and Lorenzo appeared from the dining room.

"That charlatan, Colin McCullough!" Margo announced loudly. She had everyone's attention. By this time, Olive and Burt had appeared on the balcony railing and Eve's staff had come from the kitchen to see what was going on.

"What did he do?" asked Reid.

To everyone and no one Margo said, "He stole money from me, is what he did. He needs to be arrested immediately! He tricked my husband. He tricked him, conned him! He can't have the money. It's not right!"

Everyone looked around to see if Colin was in the room and when they realized he wasn't, eyes turned to his door upstairs. As if on cue, Colin opened his door and walked to the balcony railing looking down at the crowd below.

"Get down here you thief!" Margo yelled at him.

Colin obeyed. Eve thought it strange that he didn't look angry in spite of the fact that Margo was yelling offensive things about him. Instead, he looked shocked and bewildered as he slowly walked down the stairs. When he finally descended the stairs, he walked up to Margo and said, "So, it's true? I was trying to find out but I couldn't get a hold of… But it's true? It's really true?"

"Margo looked around the room wildly. "He probably doesn't even have a horse rescue! He just says that to steal money from people!"

Colin's bewilderment turned to panic as his head flew to Reid's direction. "That's not true! I do have a horse sanctuary. I swear! Your money is going to be well spent on animals that really need it."

Margo's fury was growing. She looked at Reid and yelled, "You gave him money too? Why?" She looked back and forth from Colin's face to Reid's a few times before settling on Colin's. She said, "If you killed him, you can't have the money. Convicted murderers don't get their ill-gotten gains, right? Then it would revert to me." Margo began rapidly nodding her head. "Yes," she said as she took a deep breath. She calmed down a little and looked to Reid. "Yes. Then you could get your money back from this fraudster too, Reid."

"What's going on?" asked the sheriff, who had appeared and was walking over to Margo.

Margo was delighted to see him. "He's the murderer!" she cried as she pointed her finger at Colin. "That man murdered my husband for his life insurance policy. Arrest him!" Margo's temporary calmness disappeared. "Arrest him!" she cried. "Arrest him!"

Next thing Eve knew, she was playing mother hen, calming Margo and ushering her into the office to explain everything to Sheriff Strider. Eve's role as hysterical lady's companion awarded her the opportunity to stay in the room while the sheriff questioned Margo.

"He's a cheat and a liar. Everyone knows that. Everyone, everyone," Margo babbled as she sat down in the office chair across from the sheriff. Eve sat next to her.

"Have you known Colin for a long time?" Eve asked gently.

"No, I don't know him. I don't associate with his kind," Margo said with an air of superiority.

"Then how to do you know he's a cheat and a liar?" the sheriff asked.

"Because I know! Everyone knows!"

"How does everyone know?" the sheriff asked so slowly and calmly that it had the desired effect of slowing and calming Margo enough for her to explain.

"Because, about a year ago there was an animal fundraiser," Margo began. "Art was on the board of the foundation for years. It was a big hoodie doo, all the richest people were there to be squeezed for cash. This is in Kentucky mind you, but it was such a big event that apparently it lured even the con artists from Arizona, like Colin McCullough." She spat out his name like it was a dirty word. "He crashed the event and started working the room and telling all these philanthropists about his horse sanctuary in Arizona. He was trying to get them to give him money, the money that they were there to give to CARED— that's the name of the foundation, an acronym for Coordinated Animal Rescue Eastern Division. Obviously, the foundation did not appreciate a party crasher and Art was elected to kick him out. But my husband, always too nice, apparently got sucked into this man's lies and got him to promise him some money. Except we don't have any money, so my husband apparently took me off of his life insurance policy and put on this stupid, and probably non-existent, horse rescue in Arizona as his beneficiary. So, of course, Colin killed him. Art was so stupid, he practically deserved it."

Eve stood and physically distanced herself from Margo. It was stupid, but she was afraid of catching some evilness.

"You can arrest him now," said Margo confidently to the sheriff.

"You think that his motive for killing Dr. Wells was the life insurance money?" asked the sheriff.

Margo looked at him like he was stupid. "Absolutely. It's a million dollars."

"The life insurance money that you thought was yours?"

"Yes. But it's not. My deceitful husband changed it!"

"But you didn't know that until a few minutes ago?"

"Correct," Margo said with a steely gaze. "Are you all caught up now? Can you arrest him now?"

"Mrs. Wells, you don't seem to be grasping the concept that you have the exact same motive as Dr. McCullough."

"What? No, I don't. I'm not a professional conman."

"But you were under the impression that in the event of your husband's death, you would be rewarded with a million dollars."

"It's not a reward. I earned that money being married to such a…" Margo trailed off as the reality of the situation started to dawn on her. "I didn't do it. You don't think I did it, do you? I didn't do it. I didn't!" she shrieked. She then suddenly quieted and stared at the wall behind the sheriff. "I know who did it," Margo mumbled to the wall before she resumed her intense stare at the sheriff. Calmly and confidently, she said, "Colin did it. It has to be him. It has to. Colin McCullough has to be the one who murdered my husband."

## Chapter Nine

During the remainder of Margo's interview, the sheriff's phone pinged repeatedly with the sound of text message notifications. As it became clear that the only thing Margo had to say was about Colin's guilt, the sheriff looked more at his phone than he listened to her. Finally, he put an end to the interview and made a phone call. As he spoke with one of his deputies about a county snowplow that was out of commission, Eve escorted Margo out to the lobby. Margo made it very clear that she didn't appreciate the company. She couldn't get away from Eve fast enough. Margo walked as fast as her spiked heels and thin, short legs allowed. Everyone in the lobby, including Colin, watched Margo as she marched up to her suite and slammed her door. Everyone except Olive. Eve noticed Olive kept her gaze trained on Jessica.

Eve desperately wanted to talk to Colin. Margo may be vile, but she also might be right about Colin. Eve wanted to know what he had to say about Margo's accusation, but she refrained from approaching him. She didn't want to get in the sheriff's way. Certainly, after his phone call, his first order of business would be to interview Colin himself. She was playing a delicate dance with the sheriff on too many levels to do anything that might upset him. Eve focused her attention on Olive instead.

Eve approached Olive and asked if she would like to join her in her suite for a cup of tea. Olive seemed reluctant. Eve wondered if it was because she didn't want to leave the pool of murder suspects in case anyone did or said something telling, or if Olive simply didn't want to talk. Finally, Eve coaxed her into accepting the invitation when she leaned over and whispered, "I want to talk to you about Art."

Olive appeared distracted by her thoughts as Eve led her to the manager's suite. Upon arrival to the small kitchenette, Eve filled the electric kettle with water while she kept her eye on her guest. Olive, with eyebrows drawn together, quizzically stared at nothing as she centered herself onto one of the small café sized dining chairs. It was evident that Olive had something on her mind.

"Were you at the CARED fundraiser?" Eve asked abruptly.

"Fundraiser?" Olive asked, pulling her attention from elsewhere. "What fundraiser?"

"The CARED fundraiser about a year ago."

"Oh. Yes," Olive replied, finally focusing on Eve. "Art was on the board of CARED but I was a volunteer at the event. He always had a way of talking me into those things. Not that I minded. I'm a sucker for a good cause. Why?"

"Do you remember Colin being there?"

"Of course. It was quite the dramatic event, or so everyone thought. They all acted like a party crasher was the end of the world. People can get worked up by the littlest things, can't they? Colin wasn't disruptive or anything. Art felt so bad about kicking him out."

"So, it wasn't a common occurrence that people

crashed these fundraisers?"

"A fundraiser of that scale was not thrown often. When it was, a lot of security guards were hired. The CARED staff was very embarrassed about the breach."

"How did he do it?"

"Do what?"

"How did Colin get into the fundraiser?" Eve clarified.

"Oh," Olive titled her head. "I don't know. I never cared enough to ask."

"Why did Art kick him out? Why not one of the security guards?"

"I'm sure everyone agreed that Art would be more tactful. There was a chance that one of the hired security guards would make a scene while Art would quietly placate Colin, which he did." Olive laughed. "In fact, they became friends!"

"Margo thinks Colin is a fraudster. What do you think?"

With a sudden sour expression Olive replied, "I think that if you spot it, you got it."

"I'm sorry. I don't follow."

"Oh, it just means that if you see a fault in someone else, it is usually a fault that you yourself have."

"You think Margo is a fraudster?"

"I think she is manipulative and greedy and will do anything for money."

"And what do you think about Colin?"

"I think he seems like a nice enough guy. Yes, he crashed the event, but it was just the act of a man who was desperate to help the animals he vowed to care for. There was a lot of money walking around that room. No one would have been hurt if a little of it went to Colin. Art talked with him for a long time and Colin stayed in touch, sending him information about his sanctuary horse ranch. Art really believed in him and his vision. I trust—trusted Art. If Art trusted Colin, I trust Colin."

"Art married Margo."

Olive chuckled sadly. "Good point. Maybe I shouldn't trust everyone Art trusted."

"I overheard them talking," Eve said. "Art and Colin. I believe I heard Art say that he was going to go to Colin's horse sanctuary after the conference. Is that true?"

"Yes. That's why he asked Emily to have the conference out here. He wanted to come see Colin's ranch in person, but Art was strapped for cash so he thought if he could get a paid airline ticket out here, he could kill two birds with one stone."

"Well, that answers that question. So, you don't think that Colin killed Art?"

"I'm not ruling him out but he's not first on my list."

"Who is?"

"Margo, of course."

"Not Jessica?"

"Jessica? Why do you ask?"

"You seemed more interested in Jessica even though Margo was making a show of storming off just now."

"Jessica's face is so very familiar to me. But I can't place where I know her from, that's all. Plus, I've seen the 'Margo storming off' show so many times, the intended dramatic effect falls flat. I don't have to witness her current behavior to know that she is the most likely person to have killed poor Art."

An eerie silence settled that accentuated the sound of the electric kettle automatically clicking off. Eve poured two mugs of hot water. "She is wicked, isn't she?"

"You don't know the half of it," Olive replied, accepting her mug and the selection of tea bags. "I never understood Art and Margo. Their marriage was a scientific study in the theory that opposites attract. Take that CARED fundraiser for example. That was a perfect example of a shared interest, but it was for completely different reasons. Art wanted to help animals and Margo wanted to hobnob with the incredibly wealthy. I remember her prancing around, trying to look like she was one of them. Her desperation to fit in while wearing an old, outdated gown... I would have felt sorry for her if she wasn't so selfish and mean-spirited. She—" Olive stopped mid-sentence and gasped. She clutched her hand atop her ample bosom.

"What?" Eve asked.

"The fundraiser!"

"What about it?"

"That's where I've seen Jessica before," Olive replied with the rounded, intense eyes of realization.

"At the CARED fundraiser?"

"Yes! I remember keeping my eye on her because she kept staring across the room at Art. It was a little bizarre, a little stalkerish honestly. Nothing happened, so I wrote it off to my hyper-imagination. But now that she's here too..." Olive looked at Eve, letting her suspicious look finish her thought for her.

"Yeah. That can't be a coincidence, can it? I mean, if she's from Kentucky, why would she be at a conference in Arizona? I mean, I know you are but you were asked to come as a presenter. It seems likely all the attendees at the conference would be from around here. Why would she come to Arizona to see presenters that she could likely catch at a conference back home?"

"Maybe to see Reid?" Olive suggested. "He never does speaking engagements."

"True. But you said at the fundraiser she was staring at Art. And I caught her staring at him the whole time during his argument with Gabriel. Can you remember anything else from that fundraiser? Did she do anything that might explain her interest in Art?"

"Let's see..." Olive drummed her fingers on the table. "I remember her keeping tabs on Art with her eyes most of the evening, but then when Reid and Art walked off to a back room to have a private conversation, she followed them."

"Reid was there?"

"He's a wealthy person in the horse world. They were all there."

"And Jessica followed Art and Reid. Did she eavesdrop on their conversation?"

"No, the position was already taken."

"What?"

"I followed the mystery woman— Jessica. I was keeping a reasonable distance to avoid detection, and I assumed she was doing the same thing with the people she was following. I saw her look down the corridor and then she walked away back in the direction of the party. Like I said, I started to think I was being fanciful. I thought maybe she simply followed them thinking the restrooms were down there and realized they weren't. But I did look down the corridor myself and saw Margo with her ear up against a door."

## Chapter Ten

At the same moment that Olive and Eve were walking into the lobby after their tea, Colin and Sheriff Strider were also entering the room from the office on the opposite side. Eve and the sheriff made eye contact. Olive and Colin wandered away, dissipating in Eve's peripheral vision. She and the sheriff walked towards each other, meeting in the middle of the lobby. After reaching her desired destination— the sheriff— Eve realized they needed to relocate their meeting. She wanted to share the information that Olive had just told her and she wanted to learn whatever had transpired during Colin's interview, but they couldn't talk in the middle of the public space.

The sheriff was on the same page. He softly said, "My place?" as he nodded back to the office door. "Or yours," he added with a quick glance at the door to Eve's suite.

Eve couldn't help but giggle as she said, "Technically, they're both mine." But the temporary moment of lightheartedness vanished as she considered the implications. "The office," she replied seriously. She thought it would be more professional. She was afraid that if they went into her personal space, things might get too personal. He might feel comfortable asking her personal questions. Uncomfortable questions. Questions she didn't want to answer. Questions regarding Wes's location.

Eve followed the sheriff into the office, ignoring the stares of the lobby's inhabitants. As soon as she closed the door behind her, she told him everything that she had just learned from Olive. She let him digest the new information for a moment before asking, "What did Colin say?"

"Nothing incriminating," Sheriff Strider said as he sat down. "He said that he crashed the fundraiser hoping to find a sympathetic ear and an open checkbook. He was very disappointed to be found out before he could secure any funds for his horse sanctuary. He felt bad that he had wasted the money to fly out for nothing. But at least he had met Dr. Wells and he seemed eager to help how he could, so he tried to not think of it as a total loss."

"He does seem like a nice guy, doesn't he?" Eve suggested.

"Maybe."

"I hope he is," she said with a sigh.

"Why?"

"Because I asked Colin and Lorenzo to take care of the horses while—" Eve stopped talking abruptly, suddenly furious with herself. *Wasn't your plan to NOT talk about Wes being gone?!* she yelled at herself inside her head. She realized she needed to keep talking, to try and take that foot out of her mouth, to revert the conversation back to Colin. "While it's snowing," she said, finishing her sentence with an alternative ending. "They helped put the horses in the stables when the snow started coming down hard. So, I just hope they are both good guys since I'm letting them around my precious horses. Did Colin tell you anything interesting? Did he tell you if he knew about the life insurance?"

"The sheriff paused long and hard with a suspicious stare before answering with, "Yes, he knew. Dr. Wells had told him that the sanctuary was the new beneficiary of the policy."

"That's strange, isn't it?"

"I thought so, but Dr. McCullough said it was a show of good faith that Dr. Wells supported his vision and would do his best to help secure funds. Dr. Wells didn't have the cash to invest himself, but the one thing he could give the sanctuary was future funding in the way of his life insurance policy."

"Did you ask him how he got into the exclusive fundraiser?"

"No. Why?"

"Just wondering. It might give us an indication if he's a talented conman or just a idealistic crusader."

"Well, at the moment, I am more interested in Dr. Denmon's movements at that fundraiser."

"I'll go get her for you if you let me sit in on the interview."

Sheriff Strider smiled but remained silent. When he finally said, "fine," Eve bolted out the door before he could change his mind.

As she walked through the lobby, she heard her phone ping and stopped to get it from her pocket. It was a text from Wes. As she read it, the heaviness in her chest lightened. She took a moment to enjoy the release of crushing worry that had been weighing her down even more than she had realized. She took a deep breath of relief as she looked around the room.

Olive was in the corner, admiring a painting. Lorenzo and Kelly were sitting on one of the couches talking and laughing. Eve listened to their conversation as she drafted a text to respond to Wes. Writing texts took her longer than most. Unlike Roxie, she was not fast as lighting using a tiny electronic keyboard, and unlike almost everyone else in the world, she insisted on writing her texts in full sentences with proper spelling. The commonplace uses of "u" as a replacement for "you" and "4" as a replacement for "for" had always made her cringe. And this particular text was taking her even longer to draft because she kept pausing as her interest was diverted to Lorenzo and Kelly's discussion. At first, Eve had the thought that their giggling was inappropriate so soon after Art's death, but then she admonished herself for the thought. She was no better. And was it so bad to try and stay positive during tough times? Just because something bad happened, it didn't mean that you needed to be dragged down into depression with it. Finally, Eve considered their lighthearted banter good for the ambience and listened with amusement.

"Is that true?" Lorenzo was asking Kelly.

"Oh, yes," Kelly replied. "She's been my client for a long time. I know all sorts of things about her."

"Fascinating! Tell me more."

"She swears that she communicates with her horses."

"Like Dr. Tolliver?"

"No!" said Kelly as she flirtatiously pushed Lorenzo's shoulder. "Not like Reid! She's loony. She says they talk to her. She has told me about conversations that they've had!"

"Really?" Lorenzo asked with skepticism.

"Yes! I'm serious. Everyone who knows her knows about it, but she's too wealthy for anyone to contradict her, including me. I'm certainly not going to be the one to tell her that Lady Diamond Heart did not tell her that she loves Fuji apples but hates Gala apples."

"Aren't those basically the same apple?"

"Yes!" Kelly laughed. "And I'm sure Lady Diamond Heart doesn't have a preference. But I will not be the one to say it. I'm not losing her as a client! She pays very well. I want to stay her vet forever. I can work with crazy!"

Lorenzo kept asking Kelly questions and she easily responded to all of them. Eve was under the impression that Kelly was simply enjoying a gossip session, but that Lorenzo was manipulating the situation to get Kelly to reveal information that might be beneficial to him. Eve was also pretty sure that Olive's interest in that painting on the wall was a ruse to allow her eavesdropping on Lorenzo and Kelly's conversation. But why Olive would be interested in this particular conversation, she did not know.

Eve finished her well-crafted, clear, concise text to Wes and headed up the stairs to Jessica's room. Eve knocked and Jessica opened the door greeting Eve with a pleasant expression that immediately turned sour when she heard that she was required to come down and speak with the sheriff. She silently followed Eve down to the office.

Eve closed the office door as Jessica sat down and took the third chair in the room and set it on the side of the desk. Not on Jessica's side, but not on the sheriff's side either. She just wanted to be a fly on the wall. It didn't work. Jessica took equal turns looking defiantly at Eve and the sheriff.

"Dr. Denmon," the sheriff began. "Were you a guest at the CARED fundraiser event in Kentucky about a year ago?"

"Yes," Jessica replied directly. Eve thought it interesting that she didn't question why he had asked her the question. It was as if she was expecting it.

"Are you from Kentucky?"

"Yes."

"You were at the fundraiser and now you're here."

"That's not a crime."

"But it doesn't make sense. Only the richest people were invited to that fundraiser, not veterinarians. And why would you travel all the way to Arizona for a conference?"

"I don't see why I need to answer those questions. They have nothing to do with Arthur Wells's murder. I have nothing to do with Arthur Wells's murder. I was in my room when it happened. I have no one to corroborate that, but I don't need to because I didn't do anything wrong."

"And that's all you have to say?"

Jessica stared coldly at the sheriff for a minute. Finally she said, "I will add this... If you think that his murder was for money then I'm not a good suspect. I have money, lots of money. Yes, I am a veterinarian, but I come from a very wealthy family, and I inherited a lot of money when my parents died. It is why— to answer your earlier question— why I was an invited guest to the very exclusive CARED fundraiser."

"And why are you here at this conference?"

"Because I wanted to come to this conference. It is for horse veterinarians, of which I am one. I have every right to be here simply because I wanted to be here."

"You can certainly see why it seems like too much of a coincidence."

"Why? A lot of people here were also at that fundraiser."

"Yes, we know that Dr. Hudson was volunteering, Mrs. Wells accompanied her husband, Dr. Tolliver was there as a guest, and Dr. McCullough was a party crasher."

"There's more than that," said Jessica.

"Who?"

"I'm married, not blind. Handsome men do not go unnoticed by me," Jessica said as she stared at the sheriff a little too long for Eve's comfort.

"Go on," Eve prodded, partly to stop the quiet stare.

"Firstly," Jessica said as she looked at Eve, "the horse trainer, Lorenzo. He was the date of a well-known socialite that had been close friends with my parents. I think she had been vacationing in Arizona and brought Lorenzo back with her to be her arm candy for the fundraiser. Her selection of pretty boys in Kentucky was getting stagnant. She wanted to wear something new and shiny on her arm that night. Lorenzo was a big hit. She was very proud of herself."

"Interesting. You said 'firstly.' Does that mean there is a 'secondly'?"

"Yes. Mr. Good Looking number two. Not as smiley, shiny, and in the spotlight as Lorenzo, but still memorably attractive as he lurked in the shadows."

"Who?"

"Dr. Burt Bullock."

# Chapter Eleven

It was late and Eve realized she hadn't fed her guests dinner. She hurriedly found Esperanza to ask her to put out a late supper, but as usual Esperanza was one step ahead of her. Eve was not surprised. Esperanza always anticipated her wants and everyone else's needs.

By the time Eve found Burt standing on the veranda pensively looking out at the snow piling up around them, the dining room offered a comfort food station. Next to a mountain of freshly baked dinner rolls, labeled pots of piping hot beef stew and vegetable stew were available for anyone to help themselves. Olive and Kelly were in the corner eating and talking. Burt looked longingly at the pots as they walked by them, but Eve continued to march him to the office to meet with the sheriff.

Eve opened the office door and motioned for Burt to sit down. He obliged, but no sooner had he sat down, his stomach growled so loud it was comical.

Eve suppressed a smile as she said, "I'll get you some beef stew."

"Vegetable stew, please," said Burt. "I'm a vegetarian."

"You are?" she asked, surprised.

"Yes."

"But you're a ranch veterinarian. A vet for ranches that raise cattle for beef."

"Yes. I know."

"And you're a vegetarian?"

"Yes."

"Isn't there some conflict of interest there?"

"True, I'm a vegetarian because I love animals. I care about the cattle I care for and I don't love the end result of their life but I also know that without the industry those creatures wouldn't even exist. Generations of those cows wouldn't exist. And I know these ranchers. They treat their cattle well. Those animals have a good life before their end. And when it comes down to it, isn't that what it's all about? Quality of life. It doesn't matter how you die. It matters how you lived."

Eve looked apologetically to the sheriff for the interruption and asked him if he too would like some stew.

He gave a curt nod as he kept his eyes on Burt. "Sure. Beef. Thank you."

By the time she returned with a tray holding a plate of rolls and the two bowls of stew, they had already begun the interview. As she walked in, Burt was speaking.

"I'm embarrassed," Burt said to the sheriff as he took his bowl of stew from Eve. He greedily took a bite.

Eve set the rolls and the sheriff's bowl on the desk. Burt took a roll. The sheriff ignored the food and said, "I just asked Dr. Bullock about his last few years away from Juniper County."

"Embarrassed?" Eve said as a prompt for Burt to continue as she sat.

He took another large bite of stew as he nodded. After swallowing, he said, "I'm embarrassed that I left my simple but happy life here for money. You know, like I told you earlier," Burt directed to Eve, "the grass is always greener elsewhere. And when you live in Arizona, that becomes literal. Everywhere literally has greener grass than the wispy brown weeds we have here. And when you add the green of money into the equation…"

Eve thought Burt looked sad as he took another bite of stew. She was happy to see that the sheriff was also taking Burt's moment of contemplation to take a few bites of food as well.

"I'm embarrassed," continued Burt, "because I made a bad decision. I took a job in Kentucky with a collective that breeds and raises racehorses. It paid really well and the property I lived and worked on was green and gorgeous. I thought I had died and gone to horse heaven. But… Well, I realized I preferred it here. So, I'm back."

"Why do you prefer it here?"

"I just do."

"Why didn't you like it there?"

"I just didn't."

"Dr. Bullock…" said the sheriff with a tone of warning.

"Fine," Burt said in a hushed voice. "There are a lot of animal rights activists that hate horse racing in general but specifically hate the collective that I was working for. I don't want it common knowledge that I worked for them. I would appreciate it if you didn't tell anyone that I'm associated with them. Please."

"What is the name of the collective?"

"I'd rather not say."

"You're not in a position to bargain."

"Will you keep the information to yourself?"

"I cannot promise that," replied the sheriff.

"But if it isn't germane to the investigation, it won't come up, correct?"

"Correct."

Burt sighed. "Fine. It's called the Worthington Collective."

"We were told you were at the big CARED fundraiser

last year," Sheriff Strider said.

"Yes, I was a volunteer," Burt replied, visibly relieved at the subject change. "I needed something in my life to feel good about. Volunteering for CARED kept me sane. And that's where I met Art. We bonded."

"Bonded over what?"

"Oh, just stuff… life."

"Give me an example."

Sighed again. "Again, I respectfully ask you to keep this quiet."

"And again, Dr. Bullock, I will have no reason to bring anything up unless it is relevant to my investigations."

"I understand," said Burt with resignation. "While volunteering with Art, I mentioned my job at the Worthington Collective and, like people do, I complained about my job. Art told me that he had worked for the collective for a short time many years ago and had similar, you know, grievances, so he quit."

"And why didn't you just quit?"

"I couldn't. I couldn't quit, so instead I made the best of my time there. Meeting Art was one of the highlights. He was great. I really enjoyed volunteering at CARED with him."

Sheriff Strider gave Burt one of his signature long, hard, suspicious stares that Eve had the displeasure of enduring just a short time before. The sheriff finally broke the silence by saying, "We were told that when you were at the CARED fundraiser you were 'lurking in the shadows'."

"Lurking in the shadows?" Burt said with a short guttural laugh. "Yes, I suppose I was. That's what volunteers do. They lurk in the shadows, trying not to be seen as they orchestrate a seamless event."

"Where were you during the incident?"

"What incident? Colin getting kicked out of the fundraiser?"

"No. The tumbleweed incident. Yesterday."

"Oh," said Burt, his look of mirth completely extinguished. "I already told your deputy. I don't know."

"You don't know?"

"No. I don't know the exact moment of the incident, so I don't know where I was. I was walking around the property admiring it. Eve can vouch for me. I ran into her." He looked to Eve for confirmation. She looked back at him and then at the sheriff with undisguised discomfort by Burt's attempt to use her as his alibi.

"Did you see anyone else?"

"Margo."

"What was she doing?"

"She was on her balcony. I didn't see her at first. She was wearing that brown dress and blended in with the building. But then I saw a movement out of the corner of my eye and looked up. I saw her, but she didn't see me. I actually hid behind some trees before she could spot me. It was childish but it's always been my play with Margo. I avoid her to the best of my ability."

"Why?"

"She thinks of the humans of the world as her pool of servants. I thought if she saw me she would call down to me to bring her a glass of water or something else ridiculous like that. She's just that kind of person. And I'm the kind of stupid person that will do it."

"What time did you see Margo on her balcony?"

"I have no idea. Maybe in the middle of the time the conference ended and when I ran into Eve. Maybe a little later. Yes, later. Maybe closer to the time that I ran into Eve. But I don't know for sure. I didn't check the time."

"Tell me about Art," said the sheriff.

Burt's face brightened a little. "Art was a brilliant man, far more brilliant than he let on. Maybe not when it came to love, but when it came to science he had real talent. He was one of those child prodigies that started college when he was fourteen or fifteen. He had a degree in chemistry under his belt before he even decided that he wanted to be a veterinarian. And he was a good man. I can't believe this happened to him. I should have…"

"Should have what?"

"Oh, nothing."

"Should have what?" Sheriff Strider repeated.

"I should have told him what I thought of his wife. I should have told him to leave her. It wasn't my place, but I wish I would have done it anyway."

"You think she did this?"

"Honestly, who else could it have been? Everyone loved Art. The only one who ever had a bad word to say about the man was his wife and it's all she did."

"Why do you think he stayed with her?"

"Who knows? Perhaps it was penance for past sins. But no. I think it was just that he was a good person. He was a positive person who liked to fix problems. And she was the ultimate problem to solve. And what a problem! She was constantly berating him. Like I said, she was the only one that ever had anything bad to say about him. The more I think about it, the more I think that she has to be responsible. Plus…"

"Plus?" Eve interjected. She then followed it with an intense and silent stare. But her attempt to use the sheriff's tactic did not have the same effect.

"Nothing," was all Burt said.

"But Margo was on her balcony during the window of opportunity," the sheriff pointed out. "Not at the stables."

"So?" Burt barked, suddenly angry. "She could have just got back from doing it or just about to do it. She's very sneaky." Burt stopped talking as he looked at a spot on the floor. He was in his own world with his own thoughts. It was evident that he was done revealing any more interesting information. The sheriff had not yet said anything to indicate that the interview was over, but Eve could tell that it was. She stood quietly and walked over to the door to open it for Burt's release. As she opened the door she jumped back and gasped. She hadn't been prepared to be greeted by a rosy-cheeked face in the door jamb.

"Oh! Hi!" said Olive. "There you are! I was looking for you."

Eve looked at Olive suspiciously. She had noticed Olive sitting and talking to Henry and Kelly in the lobby when Eve and Burt had entered the office. Eve's location should not have been a mystery. Eve thought Olive must have been shamelessly eavesdropping at the door. She was sure of it when she asked, "What do you need, Olive?" and Olive's caught-off-guard reply was "Oh! Um... I... actually... Oh, well! Now I don't remember! How silly of me!"

Olive craned her neck to offer the sheriff a delightful smile. Eve wondered if the sheriff also found Olive's smile too innocent to be innocent.

"I must be tired," Olive added. "I should put myself to bed! Goodnight."

While standing in the doorway, Eve watched Olive walk away and up the stairs with Burt following a few steps behind her. She then closed the door and turned to Sheriff Strider. "Speaking of bed, what am I going to do with you?"

"Excuse me?" said the sheriff with laughing eyes.

Now it was Eve's turn to be caught off guard. "I... You know... sleeping arrangements. It's late but you can't leave. There's too much snow. I mean, maybe you could leave, but what if you couldn't make it back in the morning? You can't leave. It's too dangerous. You have to stay."

"Okay, okay. Stop begging. I'll spend the night."

"Oh no!"

"What? First you ask me to spend the night and now you don't want me to stay? Don't toy with me."

"Oh, hush," Eve said, stifling her smile. "I don't want my staff to go home either. I know they are only a couple of miles up the road but what if they got stuck and had to walk, or what if they also can't get back in the morning? I would feel better if everyone could safely stay here but we are at full capacity. All the rooms are taken."

"It's okay. We'll figure something out. It's not an emergency. We have heat, food, and water."

"And a murderer," Eve reminded him.

"I always thought you were a half glass full kind of lady. Guess I was wrong."

"Fine! A super fun slumber party and smores it is," she said with super sarcasm. "Let's go find my staff."

After much debate, sleeping arrangements were decided. Naiya would bunk with Eve so that Ramon and Esperanza could stay in Suite C. Sheila and Kelly said since both their rooms had two beds, they would be happy to share one and give the other to Roxie and Loretta. Sheriff Strider would stay on a cot in the office. Eve felt bad that he didn't get a room but Loretta made her feel better by reminding her that she had splurged on the best cots that money could buy and they never got used. The sheriff assured her that he would be fine, he had spent the night in much more uncomfortable places than in a nice warm room with fresh sheets and clean restrooms right next door. But, he added, he was interested to know if the mention of smores was simply a joke or in fact an option.

## Chapter Twelve

When Eve awoke in the morning, she tried to be as quiet as possible as she got ready. She was proud of her success in not waking Naiya and the dogs. She gently closed the door behind her and walked by Gabriel who was sitting in a large chair in the lobby engrossed in something on his tablet. She went to the dining room, poured herself a coffee, and went to sit at the reception desk.

Colin walked in from the back door and into the lobby. "Have you seen the snow?" he asked Gabriel after sitting across from him.

"Yes," Gabriel said without looking up from his tablet.

"I guess it was a surprise to everyone. It just blew in before anyone knew it was going to."

"Uh huh."

"The weather app that I use said it was supposed to be getting a little colder and partly cloudy, but that was it."

Gabriel looked at Colin over the top of this tablet. "I don't have time or use for small talk. It bores me."

"You prefer to discuss life and death matters?" Colin asked with a hint of annoyance.

"No. That's the opposite of small talk, that's big talk. I don't care for that either. Small talk is for retirees that have nothing better to do. Big talk is for college students who are trying to make sense of their place in the world. I am neither of those."

"So, that leaves what? Medium talk?"

"Yes. I like medium talk. Not small talk, not big talk, just medium talk. What's wrong with that? After all, there are a lot of subjects between weather and war."

Colin chuckled. "Okay, okay. But I still contend that sometimes the weather is interesting. I mean, come on, hurricanes, tornadoes, and surprise snowstorms that trap you in isolated hotels with strangers who only like medium talk. Those are interesting."

Eve saw that Gabriel smirked in Colin's general direction. She supposed that was his version of a friendly smile. "I suppose they are," he said.

Colin looked proud to have garnered the agreement of the devil's number one advocate.

Eve returned her attention to her computer to check the weather. She too thought a snowstorm that trapped people at her hotel was interesting, overly so, considering there was a murderer among the trapped. As beautiful as the snow was, she was eager to see her precious Arizona sunshine come out with a vengeance to melt it away clearing the roads and her hotel.

A quick blur in Eve's peripheral vision made her eyes dart upward and suddenly Olive was there, brimming with excitement. She leaned in and whispered, "Alright, here's what I've found out so far that you can pass along to your sheriff friend—"

"Let's go into my office," Eve said as she looked over at Colin and Gabriel to see if they had overheard. If they had heard, they were pretending they hadn't. Gabriel was once again engrossed in his tablet and Colin had picked up a magazine and was reading. "Wait, we can't use my office. The sheriff is in there sleeping, and Naiya is sleeping in my suite." Eve looked around trying to think of the best place to have a private conversation when her two regular places were taken. "The basement," Eve whispered. "Follow me."

Olive followed Eve down the basement steps and as soon as they reached the bottom, she started talking fervently. "Kelly said that it is common knowledge down in, oh what did they call it? The valley? Yes, I think it's the valley. You know, down in the Phoenix area, is that what they call it?"

"Yes."

"Kelly said that it's common knowledge that Lorenzo will do anything for money. He has very expensive tastes and gets creative when it comes to padding his paycheck."

"Are you suggesting that someone hired Lorenzo to kill Art?"

"No, I was just thinking…"

"What?"

"When we were in the stables with Art, did you smell anything?"

"Smell anything?" Eve asked with confusion.

"Yes. Anything strange, well, not strange. Did you smell anything that shouldn't have been there?"

"No. Did you?"

"No."

"Then why did you ask me that?" Eve asked with even more confusion.

"It's nothing. Never mind. But listen, I did have a thought. I wonder if maybe someone wanted to scare Art and the tumbleweed trick was only meant to frighten him, maybe into doing something for them, but it got out of control. Whoever did it could have been horrified when it ended the way it did."

"So, who do you think that might be?"

"Well, that's the question, isn't it? But, honestly, I keep coming back to Margo."

"Me too. But she certainly doesn't seem horrified. She doesn't even seem sad."

"True. Maybe she is masking her guilt with anger. Maybe she meant to do it and has no remorse. I don't know. It was just a theory."

"I keep wondering why Margo even came to this conference," said Eve. "You know her. Is this a common thing? For her to come to conferences with Art?"

"No. It is not. Margo's motivations are completely selfish. If she is here, there has to be a reason that benefits her."

"Like killing her husband?"

"Or scaring him, or trying to cause an accident. I don't know," Olive raised her hands in frustration. Then her expression quickly changed back to one of excitement. "But, that's not all I've found out."

Olive paused, suddenly looking reticent to share, so Eve prompted her. "Okay, what did you find out?"

"Well… I asked around about the horse racing collective Burt worked for, the Worthington Collective."

"I suppose this is information you learned when you were eavesdropping during Burt's official interview with the sheriff?"

"Yes," Olive said with a momentary look of contrition before her excitement was restored. "I made some calls—luckily Kentucky is in a later time zone or my friends would have been angry with me for waking them up—and…" Olive paused again, seemingly for dramatic effect.

"And?"

"I found out that one of their main investors is none other than Gabriel Spurlock."

"Well, I guess that's interesting," Eve said contemplatively, "but does it have anything to do with Art?"

"I don't think so, at least, I don't know. But that started me thinking more about Gabriel and why he's here. So, I did a little digging and I also found out that Gabriel asked to be a speaker at this conference."

"So?"

"So that's strange. Henry told me that Gabriel is a well-known professional presenter. Apparently, Gabriel typically gets paid well for speaking engagements at conferences. He's arrogant as all get out but I must admit that he is a very good presenter. But this time he asked to speak at this conference and he offered to do it for free. That is very suspicious, don't you think?"

Eve thought about Gabriel's polished speaking style. He did seem very professional, very persuasive. He put on a good show and knew it. And he didn't strike Eve as the kind of man who would sell himself short by giving away his skills for free. "Yes," agreed Eve, "that is suspicious. "Did Art and Gabriel know each other?"

"Not that I know of," said Olive. "But Art could be secretive about things sometimes."

Eve tilted her head as she regarded Olive.

"What is it?" Olive asked.

"Speaking of Art," Eve replied. "Don't you think you should be grieving him? I mean, Naiya and I just met the man and we are both really upset about his death. You were his partner for years. You were really close. You should allow yourself time to be sad. I know it's not my place, but I just feel like you aren't grieving."

"You're right. I'm not."

"But shouldn't you be?" Eve asked.

"No. Not yet. I will. Don't worry. After I figure out who killed Art, I will grieve. I can compartmentalize. I can set aside the sadness while I work. Right now, I need to find his murderer. I need to do that for Art. You understand, don't you?"

"Yes," Eve said begrudgingly. "I think I do. But just make sure not to step on the sheriff's toes. This is his investigation, not yours."

"What can I say? The early bird gets the worm and I'm up early so I'm getting all the worms. That's what he gets for sleeping in."

"Olive. I'm serious. Don't do anything dangerous, okay?"

"Oh, I'm just covering my bases. I don't think there's anything to worry about. After all, it was probably Margo. She's not going to try to kill me too."

"You really think it's her?"

"Don't you?"

"Maybe. I don't know. Burt said she saw her on her balcony which gives her story about being in her room some credence."

"She was on her balcony?"

"Yes, but he only saw her for a moment and she could have come and gone before or after that. Henry, Kelly, and Sheila were in the lobby the whole time but they weren't particularly paying attention to everyone's comings and goings.

"What room is hers?"

"Suite B."

"Does her balcony have a view of the stables?"

"Yes, it probably has the best view. Why? Do you think she saw something?"

"Like when Art made his way to the stables and she saw her opportunity? Maybe," Olive said distractedly as she waved goodbye at Eve and started up the stairs. "I'm going to see how many more worms I can get."

Eve followed Olive up the basement stairs with a smile on her face. She couldn't help it. She liked Olive. But then her smile suddenly disappeared as Eve wondered if Olive's lack of grieving was evidence of something nefarious. Like the sheriff said, her desire to help with the investigation might simply be a smokescreen. Eve reminded herself to take Olive's proffered intel with a grain of salt.

As soon as Olive opened the door to the lobby she said, "Oh my!"

Eve gently nudged Olive out of the way so that she

could see what had happened. Olive attempted to help by pointing, but it was unnecessary. Eve would have noticed the scene all by herself. After all, Margo was on the floor at the base of the east staircase yelling.

"OW!" Margo cried. "Those stupid stairs are uneven. They made me trip. They're dangerous!" Colin was at her side attempting to help her up but Margo was waving him away like he was the plague. "Keep your dirty, thieving hands off me! You can't steal my money and then pretend to be nice."

Gabriel had not bothered to get up from his seat to offer Margo help. Lorenzo was standing in the corner, watching the show but showing no interest in getting involved. Olive also stood motionless next to Eve. Eve supposed that they all didn't rush over to Margo's side for the same reason she didn't. It was hard to give Margo Wells sympathy.

Reid appeared on the balcony and hurried down the stairs. He offered Margo his hand. Margo took it while she said, "Thank you. Finally, someone bothered to help!" As she got on her feet, she again yelled, "OW!"

"What hurts?" asked Reid kindly.

Eve started to think maybe Colin was right, maybe Reid Tolliver was a saint. After all, she couldn't even force herself to pretend to be nice to Margo, and it was her job to be nice to her hotel guests. Eve knew Reid didn't like Margo either and yet here he was, showing compassion to an injured woman. Eve was impressed.

"My ankle," Margo said as she limped to the couch with Reid's help. She plopped herself down on the couch.

Reid cupped his hands around Margo's ankle. "It feels like it's swelling a little. But it's just a twist, not a break," he assured the crowd of onlookers.

Margo projected across the room to Eve, "I can't climb those stairs. I need a downstairs room."

Eve took a deep breath and walked over to Margo with as much graciousness as she could muster. "We only have the one," explained Eve. Margo opened her mouth to say something, but Eve cut her off by saying, "I'll make arrangements so you can move into it."

"Good," Margo said. "Someone will need to pack my things for me and bring them down."

"I'm aware of that," Eve said, trying to keep a neutral tone.

Eve went to the kitchen to tell Esperanza and Ramon that if they were all trapped in the hotel for another night, they would be moving up to Suite B. She then found Loretta and Roxie and asked them to clean the room and pack Margo's things and bring them downstairs. Eve was always proud of her staff's capable work, but she was particularly happy with their speed and efficiency as they quickly moved Margo into her new room. It was in everyone's best interest to keep Margo from residing in the common area. It was clear that no one wanted her around.

## Chapter Thirteen

After getting Margo moved into her downstairs suite, Eve decided to reward herself with five minutes of quiet coffee on the couch. Everyone else that was awake had gravitated into the dining room leaving the lobby deserted. But she only had a moment of alone time before Reid appeared.

"May I join you?" he asked as he flashed a confident smile.

Eve again couldn't help but feel flattered by receiving the focused attention of Dr. Reid Tolliver. "Of course," she replied sweetly.

"I like your piano," he said as he sat quite close to her.

"Thank you!" Eve said, as she turned to admire her newest antique acquisition. She was overjoyed that someone else had noticed its beauty. "I just bought it a few weeks ago at an estate sale. It's an early Steinway & Sons upright. Isn't it gorgeous? I don't play myself, but I was so excited about having it available for guests to play. Unfortunately, no one has given it much notice." She turned back to face Reid as she asked, "Do you play?"

He leaned in even closer. "Yes, in fact, I do."

"Would you play it sometime? Not now, it's too early. But perhaps later? I've been so looking forward to hearing the hotel filled with its music."

"Certainly," said Reid with a mischievous grin. "I would be honored to tickle your ivories."

Eve quickly remined herself that Reid was a murder suspect and abruptly repositioned herself on the couch, sitting sideways to put some distance in between the two of them and facing Reid straight on. She asserted a professional demeanor as she said, "So, tell me about why you and Art ended your partnership."

"Poor Art," he said as his smile faded. With far away eyes, he said, "I knew him when he was a different person. When he was younger, he was driven. Smart, talented, cocky…" Reid coughed out a sad chuckle. "He thought he could solve all the world's problems. Well, all the world's horse problems. He was a fairly arrogant young man."

"I can't see Art being like that," said Eve.

"We both were," said Reid. "That's why we were friends. But, I think there's a point in everyone's life that knocks the bravado and confidence out of us. One thing that shatters our hopeful view of the world, that changes us, that makes us realize that we are only human and can only do so much."

"And that's when you grow up," suggested Eve.

"Exactly," said Reid looking into her eyes.

"You seem very confident," said Eve. "You don't appear to have had it knocked out of you."

"I fake it just like every other grown-up," he said as his smile returned.

"So, you had your youthful bravado knocked out of you too?"

"Yes. In fact, Art and I experienced that moment together. You'd think that it would have brought us closer together, but it didn't. We handled it very differently. It caused us to grow apart. That's what caused our partnership to come to an end."

"Margo said it was because a horse died. A girl's horse?"

"The girl's parents owned the horse but the girl was beside herself with grief. She made things very difficult, calling us up and screaming at us, following us and yelling at us while we were at other clients' homes. Art was having a hard enough time with the horse's death. He didn't need the extra emotional haranguing of a spoiled rotten teenage girl on top of it. Her parents fired us. For me, losing that job working for the Laberges was devastating. But for Art, it was losing the horse. He felt responsible, but he wasn't. I know for a fact he wasn't. Fearless— that was the horse's name— was just too sick, too weak. It wasn't Art's fault. I wish he could have realized that. We both changed that day but Art's metamorphosis was severe. He became a serious and cautious man."

"And altruistic?"

"Overly altruistic in my opinion," said Reid.

"In Margo's also," said Eve.

Reid laughed. "Well, that's not saying much. I think altruism is Margo's sworn enemy."

"Do you think she could have killed her husband?"

"Yes."

"Wow. No hemming or hawing? Just, 'yes'?"

Reid looked at Eve seriously and intently. "I've known Margo longer than anyone else here and I am being completely honest when I tell you that Margo Wells is not a good person. She most definitely could have killed her husband. I'm not saying she did and I'm not saying she didn't. I'm simply saying she could have."

Eve was well aware that people lied. They lied to keep secrets. They lied to make themselves look better or to make someone else look worse. And sometimes they lied for no good reason. But Eve truly believed that at this moment, Reid was being completely honest with her. Of course, it wasn't a stretch of the imagination believing that Margo was a bad person. "So, you and Art had a falling out years ago, but you were friends again. You made up. Isn't he the one who asked you to come out here to Arizona to be a speaker at this conference?"

"Yes. All correct. You know your stuff."

"Not everything. I'm interested to know how you and Art reconnected."

"Oh, it was, I don't know, about a year ago I think. We ran into each other at a fundraiser. He was running it, I was supporting it. I hadn't seen him in years. We spoke and cleared the air and became friendly again." Reid's face transformed into grimness as he said, "It's so sad. I just got my old friend back and now he's gone."

Eve and Reid shared a moment of quiet, serious contemplation until the chatter from the dining room got louder. Olive, Jessica, Sheila, and Kelly walked into the lobby.

"Ow," Olive said as she readjusted the side of her bosom.

"Come on in ladies," said Reid. "Join us. Make yourselves comfortable."

"Thank you for the invitation," Olive said as she walked towards them and sat down, "but, unfortunately, we ladies can never make ourselves truly comfortable."

"And why is that?"

"Bras. Women are always uncomfortable because wearing a bra is uncomfortable but not wearing a bra is also uncomfortable. It's six or half a dozen discomfort-wise."

"And each bra is its own special brand of discomfort," added Kelly.

"True!" said Olive.

Sheila sat on the other side of Reid, crossed her legs and leaned in toward him as she engaged him in a quiet, intimate conversation. Eve felt uncomfortable, like she was a piece of bread on a Reid sandwich. Roxie was walking by with a large clear plastic cup filled with something purple and looked at the three of them. Eve felt even more uncomfortable. She took the last sip of her coffee and stood.

Eve's assumption that Roxie was analyzing their awkward placement on the couch was wrong. As usual, Roxie has her own priorities and interests.

"I like your tattoo," said Roxie and she pointed to the sun tattoo on Sheila's ankle.

"Oh, please don't," Sheila laughed. "I wish I would have never got the silly thing."

"That's what Bridget always says too," Roxie said. "She's a lady who works here. She's always trying to talk me out of getting one. She says she regrets all her tattoos. She calls herself a… What is it, Eve?"

"A cautionary tale," Eve replied.

"Yeah, that," said Roxie. "But it's like she got to do all the fun stuff just so she can tell me not to do it. I don't think that sounds fair and I really want to get a tattoo. I just don't know what yet, but I have lots of ideas."

"Oh, honey, don't do it," said Olive. "I see all these beautiful young women these days with tattoos all over their bodies and all I want to do is take the scratchy side of a kitchen sponge and scrub them clean."

"I have to agree," said Jessica. "I only have one tattoo and I also wish I didn't get it."

"What is it?" Roxie asked.

"Many years ago, I lost someone very close to me and while I was grieving, I decided to get his likeness tattooed on my forearm. At the time, it seemed like a nice tribute and a way to make my parents mad but now I regret it. And now I have to always wear long-sleeved shirts. I've spent more time hiding it than I ever did enjoying it."

"But I'm not going do something like that," Roxie said. "I want something artistic, something pretty. Body art is just art that is on your body," she added with an air of wisdom.

"Do you remember a picture that you had on your wall when you were little?" Kelly asked Roxie.

"What do you mean?" asked Roxie.

"My thing was unicorns," Kelly said. "Everywhere in my childhood room was unicorns."

"Oh, yeah," Roxie laughed. I had princesses. I loved princesses."

"Would you want a big tattoo of a princess?"

"No! Of course not! I'm not a kid anymore."

"See? Tastes change."

"But that was when I was little. I'm an adult now."

"You're a young adult. Don't you think that your tastes might change in 5, 10, or 20 years and you might regret your tattoo choice?"

Roxie paused and thought for a moment. "No. I know what I like."

"Oh really?" said her mother's voice behind Roxie.

Roxie's head whipped around to face Loretta. "Yeah. Really."

"This coming from the girl who redecorates her room every six months!" Loretta said to the group.

"You can't redecorate your body every six months," Olive said.

"Exactly," Eve offered despite the dangers of piling onto to Roxie and getting on her bad side. "I've always felt like getting a tattoo was tantamount to a commitment to wear the same hat or shoes for the rest of your life. Why would you want to do that? Don't you want to have a clean slate so that you can change your look? Tattoos are just a bad decision for fashion."

Roxie stared down her nose at Eve with a perturbed expression. Eve braced herself for a comeback. As a woman who obviously dressed for comfort and not for fashion, she had left herself wide open to criticism. But instead of making a comment about Eve having no right to make such an argument, Roxie took a sip of her thick, creamy, purple drink.

"Roxie!" Eve said as she remembered that shade of purple. "Is that a milkshake? Are you drinking a milkshake for breakfast?"

"It's a smoothie," said Roxie, taking another sip/bite of the creamy thickness.

"Is it made with the berry ice cream we just got?" Eve asked.

"Yes."

"Then it's a milkshake!"

"It has berries it in. It's healthy. And whatever! It's hella yummy!"

"But it's snowing," said Sheila. "And you're eating ice cream?"

"I love eating ice cream when it's snowing!" Roxie said with a big grin. "It's the best! I love eating something cold when it's cold. I'm just weird I guess," she added proudly.

"Well, I suppose eating ice cream for breakfast in the cold weather is a better way to show your individuality than getting a tattoo," Olive offered.

"Really," said Jessica. "With everyone getting tattoos these days, it's pretty commonplace. It doesn't show any individuality at all. It's almost more subversive and cool to not get a tattoo."

Roxie's smile faded as she turned away from the group and quietly continued on her way to the basement with some obligatory head shaking. Roxie let her body language let them all know that they were old and just didn't get it.

Loretta followed her daughter after whispering, "Thanks!" to the ladies of the anti-tattoo league.

Eve had been so enthralled with the conversation that she hadn't noticed that the office door had opened. Sheriff Strider stood in the doorway with an adorable case of bed head. She couldn't help but wonder how long he had been standing there. Was it pre or post Reid sandwich?

## Chapter Fourteen

"Good morning. How did you sleep?" Eve asked the sheriff after she walked over to greet him.

"Well. Too well," he added with embarrassment. "I didn't expect to sleep this long. That cot is more comfortable than my own bed."

"You're not the only one," Eve said as she watched the door to her own suite open. "Naiya just made her appearance also."

The sheriff mumbled something in response, but Eve wasn't paying attention. She was trying to remember the contents of her medicine cabinet as she watched Naiya walk across the lobby to the dining room. Sheriff Strider said something else before he walked to the men's room, but Eve couldn't concentrate on anything other than how red and raw Naiya's nose looked. It must be painful, she thought. Reid had been complaining that his allergies were causing his nose to hurt but his didn't look nearly as bad as Naiya's, and she had a much darker complexion. The tip of her nose was truly inflamed as a result of her constant crying on top of her allergies. Eve was pretty sure that she had some medicated ointment that would help.

As Eve walked across the lobby to her suite to find the ointment, she noticed that Lorenzo had appeared and was in the corner looking at the same painting Olive had been looking at yesterday. On the surface, his casual stance appeared innocent enough, but Eve found it suspicious and wondered if he too was using the convenient location to eavesdrop on the others in the lobby.

By the time Eve found some ointment in her medicine cabinet for her friend's frightful nose, Naiya had returned to the suite with a cup of coffee and sat at the small café table in Eve's kitchenette.

"You've got it made," said Naiya as Eve walked over to join her. "You don't even have to make your own coffee in the morning."

Eve placed the ointment on the table and motioned to her nose as sign language. "Yes, I don't have to make my coffee, but I have to walk through a room full of people to get it. So, first I have to get dressed and make sure I don't look a complete mess. It's always a decision to be made. Stay in my pajamas and make my own coffee or get cleaned up and dressed– without the aid of caffeine— and walk through a possibly crowded room to get my coffee."

"And today, you have to walk through a room full of potential murderers," Naiya said with serious contemplation.

"Which is something I prefer to do when I'm not groggy. It's best to be alert in that situation," Eve said with a lighthearted smile. She wanted to keep Naiya's spirits up. "How are you doing? You look like you've been crying again. Your nose is so raw. Hopefully, this ointment will help."

"Yes. I know. I'm sorry."

"You don't need to be sorry."

"Yes, I do," said Naiya as she opened the ointment and applied some to her nose. "I've been so self-obsessed thinking this is all about me, about my feelings. I should be thinking about poor Art and the people that actually knew him and loved him."

"Well, don't count Margo in that group."

"I wasn't." Naiya gasped and looked scared. "What about Blaze? I can't believe I forgot about him! He was supposed to be my patient and I completely forgot about his well-being. I'm an awful person and a terrible vet. Did they take him away? Is he going to be put d—" she stopped as the word caught in her throat. Naiya looked as if she was on the precipice of another crying fit.

"No, it's fine! Don't cry! He's fine!"

"He is?" Naiya asked hopefully.

"Yes. He's totally fine."

"Really?"

"Yes, really."

Naiya calmed herself and took a deep breath. "What happened?"

"Can you keep a secret?" Eve asked.

"Yes."

"Wes took him. I didn't know what I was doing, but I just had Wes drive him out of here before I called anyone. Luckily, he got out of the area without getting caught in the snowstorm. I didn't know where he was going to take Blaze but I just needed him to get as far away from here as possible. I was just so scared about what might happen to him."

"So, Blaze and Wes are on the run with nowhere to go?"

"No. Reid saved the day and quickly secured a new tumbleweed free home for him in Tennessee. I was asking Colin if Blaze could take refuge at his sanctuary but Colin reminded me that it's in Arizona and has more tumbleweeds than here. Then Gabriel said that it would be a good idea to get him as far away as possible. That's when Reid stepped in suggesting that he use his many connections to find Blaze a new home. It was amazing, the very first person he called agreed to take him."

"Do you really think there is going to be a manhunt,

or you know, horse hunt for Blaze?"

"I don't know, but I figured getting him across state lines, and then a few more state lines, couldn't hurt."

"Wow. So, you're like a criminal now? What does the sheriff think about this?"

"Remember when I asked you if you could keep a secret? Who do you think I meant we weren't telling?"

"Oh, that's not good. You're going to damage your relationship with him. He might not be able to forgive you."

"I know. I thought about that. But if he took Blaze away to be killed, I would certainly never be able to forgive him. I just couldn't give him the opportunity. As soon as Blaze came to this property, I felt responsible for him. I needed to take care of him. It was my job to protect him. You get it, don't you?"

"Of course. Just because we don't have children doesn't mean we don't have fierce maternal instincts. Our animals are the recipients of our unconditional love."

"Exactly. So, I just couldn't let the sheriff take him. I couldn't."

"So, you lied to him?"

"Technically, at the time I didn't lie to him. He asked me if I knew where Blaze was and I said I didn't. And I didn't know exactly where he was at that point. I didn't even know which direction Wes drove. Technically, I didn't know where they were."

"Really?" Naiya laughed. "You are citing your lack of GPS coordinates? That's thin."

"I know but that's all he asked. He didn't press the issue and I think that was by design. He could have asked more questions but he didn't. I think we understood each other. I didn't want to lie to him and he didn't want to make me lie to him. I think we're good."

"I hope so."

Eve didn't want to have this conversation. She felt an unexpected anxiety at the prospect of losing her friendship with Sheriff Strider. She made an excuse to leave, saying that she needed to get back to work. As soon as she left her suite, she heard Margo call out her name.

"Eve!" Margo called out again, even louder. "I need to use your paper shredder."

Eve took a deep breath before answering. "Sorry, Margo, but it broke last week and I haven't replaced it yet."

Margo screeched an unpleasant noise of angry frustration and limped away. Eve looked down at Margo's noticeable sparkly gold spiked heels and wondered why she was wearing them while she had a hurt ankle. Yes, they were beautiful, but there were times when fashion needed to take a back seat to comfort, and medical need. Then Eve wondered if there was indeed a medical need at all. She wondered if Margo's limp had changed. She thought she had been favoring the other leg earlier. And since Eve was wondering so many things about Margo, she once again wondered why Margo even came on this trip with her husband. Suddenly, there was a voice and an ice cream cone next to her.

"I looked them up," whispered the voice. "Twelve hundred dollars."

Eve looked to see that the voice and the ice cream cone belonged to Roxie. Roxie was standing so close to her that when Eve turned her head, her nose almost landed in the scoops of ice cream. "What's twelve hundred dollars?"

"The cost of those shoes."

"That's crazy! That can't be true."

"According to the internet, it is."

"Oh, and the internet is always right?"

"Maybe not about everything but I think it's pretty serious about shoe prices."

"Yes, that's probably the one thing the internet prioritizes." Eve looked again at the ice cream cone. "More ice cream, Roxie?" she said with equal amounts of disapproval and jealousy.

"There's still snow, so I'm still eating ice cream!" said Roxie with delight. "Plus, Mom drank half of my milkshake. Do you want some?"

"No. I mean, yes, I want some, but I can't have ice cream every time I want it. I don't have the metabolism that I had 20 years ago. Enjoy it while you can, Roxie."

"I will!" Roxie said as she bounced off towards the dining room to clean up after breakfast.

Eve was suddenly struck with the sound of silence. The lobby was devoid of people, and she didn't hear voices coming from the dining room either. She followed Roxie into the dining room and realized she was correct. It too was empty. "Where is everyone?" Eve asked.

"I guess in their rooms unless they like walking out in the snow, but who would want to do that? Oh, and Jessica is in the kitchen helping Esperanza. She said she was bored."

Eve walked into the kitchen and found Jessica looking very out of place wearing an apron and chopping onions.

Esperanza guiltily looked at Eve and said, "She said she wanted to help."

"I heard," Eve replied to Esperanza. To Jessica, she said, "You're bored enough to chop onions?"

"I know. But I'm tired of talking to all the other veterinarians and I'm tired of reading. I needed a change of scenery and company. I've never been one to cook, so for me a kitchen is like an exotic locale and chopping onions is like an adventure down the Amazon." Jessica smiled as she continued to ineptly chop onions.

"Dear," Esperanza addressed Jessica with a concerned expression, "you may want to roll up your sleeves before you continue. I don't want you getting onion on your lovely blouse. Raw onion is one of those smells that is very hard to get rid of."

"Oh, okay," Jessica said pleasantly. "Normally I wouldn't care, but who knows how long we are going to be stuck here. I might have to make these clothes last longer than I expected." She went to the sink to wash her hands.

"I know!" said Esperanza. "Poor Dr. Tolliver didn't expect it to be this cold and only brought one sweater. And Mr. Dominguez said that he didn't expect to be looking after horses and mucking out stables, his poor fancy snakeskin boots are a mess. I told him we could clean them the best we could but I don't know a lot about snakeskin boot care. And I offered him some rubber boots from the basement but he said no thanks." Esperanza giggled. "I think he'd rather look good and ruin his boots than be caught dead in a pair of loaner galoshes! Anyway, my point, honey, is that if you need some laundry done, just let us know."

"Thank you, Esperanza," said Jessica as she dried her hands. "You are so sweet." She looked at Eve as she asked, "You asked Lorenzo to care for the horses?"

"Yes, Colin and Lorenzo."

"Where's your horse wrangler? I thought he lived on site. Isn't he the beautiful bartender you had serving us the other night at the wine tasting room? Wes, I think his name was. I talked to him for a little bit. Nice guy."

"He, um, had to leave unexpectedly."

Jessica looked at Eve knowingly. "Like, leave unexpectedly with a horse trailer?"

Eve didn't say anything. She didn't want yet another questionable confidant.

Jessica nodded her head in an approving way. "Okay. I was wondering. Good. Very good. I think I like you, Eve."

Eve was flustered and didn't know what to say. "So… um…"

"It's okay, Eve," said Jessica with a smile. "I'm a 'four legs good, two legs bad' person too."

Eve appreciated the *Animal Farm* reference and the encouraging camaraderie but still felt uncomfortable and wanted to change the subject. Finally, she came up with,

"You said that you were sick of talking to the others here. Do you not like the other vets?"

"Oh, some of them are fine," replied Jessica as she rolled up her sleeves to her elbows. "But others I could do without."

"Like?" Eve asked.

"Like Gabriel Spurlock. Ugh. He's always lurking around with a permanent scowl. I find it off putting." Jessica picked up her knife and resumed her onion chopping. "I know that I can be very emotional, perhaps too emotional, but at least I have range. I have ups and downs. He's just always a pit of brooding darkness. He gives me the creeps."

"I heard that he asked to come to this conference and offered to speak for free. Do you know anything about that?"

"That's interesting," said Jessica as she paused with her knife in the air. "Has the sheriff asked him about that?"

"No, not yet. Why? Do you think it means something?"

"I think that man seems motivated by money and money alone. All he seems to do is check on his investments, and you know — scowl. If he offered to come here for free, there must be a different financial reward that was awaiting him here."

"You think so?"

"I may be clueless when it comes to cooking," Jessica said as she looked down at her pieces of onions in varying sizes and shapes, "but, unfortunately, I am very knowledgeable when it comes to the maneuvers of the greedy."

Eve decided to go suggest to the sheriff that they speak with Gabriel as soon as possible. She excused herself and on her way out, she noticed the horse tattoo on Jessica's forearm.

## Chapter Fifteen

As Eve walked to the office she couldn't stop thinking about what Naiya said. Was her decision to relocate Blaze going to ruin her relationship with the sheriff? She hadn't really let herself consider the implications. He might never forgive her. He might never trust her again. He might never talk to her again. She couldn't imagine a world where he wasn't in her life. She never imagined that they would have an abrupt falling out. The thought frightened her.

Of course, in the back of her mind, she had considered that their relationship might change one day but she always thought it would change for the better. She thought they might become closer. But even that had filled her with worry because it might not work out and she might lose her friendship with him. And she really liked her friendship with him. She didn't want to lose that.

She considered coming clean. Deceit did not come naturally to her. But telling the truth might blow it all up. She wanted things to stay good between them. Perhaps taking a step back and keeping her distance right now was the best way to preserve their friendship.

By the short time it took her to make it to the office, all she had decided on was that she was going to procrastinate having the conversation for as long as possible. She found the sheriff in the office eating his breakfast and she decided to engage in a little light banter while he ate. But even after he finished eating, she continued the small talk longer than she had expected. She wanted to hold onto these moments of pleasantness between them before she had to face the music.

Finally, she got around to telling him what she had learned from Jessica and suggested they question Gabriel concerning his reason for being at the conference. He agreed. They were on the same page. For now.

Eve found Gabriel easily enough. He, Reid, and Colin were all sitting separately in the lobby. Gabriel was on his laptop, Reid was reading a magazine, and Colin was scrolling through screens on his phone.

As Eve approached, Gabriel grunted, "Ugh."

"Bad news?" Colin asked him.

"Yes. One of my investments is going south. I had to move some money around," said Gabriel. "I recently fired my assistant, so I have to do everything myself. It's very tiresome."

"Then you shouldn't have fired your assistant," Colin said.

"It wasn't my fault," Gabriel replied slowly with a serious stare over his half moon reading glasses. "He's the one who made the mistake of thinking I find criticism constructive," he added pointedly.

Reid laughed. "You're not a fan of criticism either?"

"No, I'm not. But I am a big fan of yours," said Gabriel said to Reid. "You've made me a lot of money. I always bet on the horses you are treating. Of course, I'm not the only one and the odds aren't exuberant, but I consistently make money and I like consistently making money."

Reid laughed again. "Who doesn't? I also always bet

on the racehorse that I'm treating. I know my methods of empowerment work. Therefore, I bet heavily on my current patient. When he wins a race I am rewarded on multiple levels, with the satisfaction of a job well done and with extra money."

"I guess that's what I should have been doing this whole time," said Colin. "Betting on you, Reid!"

Reid offered a polite smile to Colin and Eve took the opportunity to interrupt the conversation. When she requested Gabriel's attendance in the office, she was given one of his signature scowls. *Point for Jessica*, Eve thought.

As Gabriel stood, Eve smelled the strong scent of sandalwood and clove. She turned her head and was not surprised to find Lorenzo. She hadn't noticed his presence when she walked in. He was once again standing in the corner, partially hidden by the west staircase. This time, he was admiring the shelves of silver antiques. She couldn't put her finger on what made his behavior seem so suspicious. She felt like he was up to something, like he was keeping tabs on everyone. She laughed to herself as she thought that if he was attempting to go unnoticed and blend into his surroundings, that purple shirt was not doing him any favors.

After Eve shut the office door behind them, Gabriel sat in the chair across from the sheriff while maintaining his resting scowl face.

The sheriff got right to the point. "Dr. Spurlock, were you asked to be a presenter at this conference, or did you ask to be a presenter?"

"Yes," Gabriel said as his expression transformed into an almost smile. It was a look of arrogant respect, as if he was finally being challenged by a worthy opponent. "I asked Emily if I could be a speaker at this conference."

"Why?" asked the sheriff.

"You seem to already know."

"Do I?"

"I wanted to meet Arthur Wells."

"Interesting. Thank you. I did not know that."

"Oh," Gabriel said with a hint of embarrassment.

"Why did you want to meet Dr. Wells?"

"Why not?"

The sheriff repeated his question, "Why did you want to meet Dr. Wells?"

Gabriel looked at the sheriff, then at Eve, and again at the sheriff before answering. "I heard he was working on something, something that might interest me as both a scientist and an investor."

"What was it?"

"I'm not sure exactly."

"How is that possible?"

"He was very secretive about it."

"Then how did you hear about this?"

"A little birdie told me."

The sheriff stared at him.

Gabriel stared back. Finally, Gabriel said, "I heard that he was going to reveal it at this conference. I was hoping that I could put a bug in his ear before then and work out something that might be financially beneficial for the both of us before he made it public. I wanted to invest."

"Invest in a mysterious thing that you knew nothing about?"

"I had it on good authority that it was a lucrative opportunity."

"From the little birdie?"

"Yes."

"And who is this birdie?"

"I am not prepared to divulge that information at this time."

"A friend of yours?"

"No. I don't have friends. It was a stranger. Simply someone who had heard of my successful financial reputation and reached out to me."

"Had you met Dr. Wells before?"

"Never. But I had heard of him. He is known to be a highly intelligent and respected veterinarian."

"Did you attend a CARED fundraiser about a year ago?"

"Certainly not. I don't do fundraisers. I make money, I don't give it away."

Eve decided that Gabriel Spurlock no longer reminded her of a college professor. She was getting more of a spy movie villain vibe from him. She was so taken aback by his undisguised greed she forgot she was supposed to be quiet and blurted out, "Wow!" It came out loud and very judgmental.

"Not giving my money to charity doesn't make me a bad person," said Gabriel. "And you shouldn't make the mistake of thinking that someone who does give their money to charity is a good person. I know those people that attend those charity events. Jackals. All of them."

"Not all of them," Eve said defensively.

"All of them," he repeated decisively.

Eve felt bad for derailing the sheriff's interview and thought she should try to help get it back on track before she pinched her lips. "If your plan was to cozy up to Art, why start such a contentious argument about immersion therapy?" she asked.

"Oh, that was nothing."

"Everyone in the room thought it was something," Eve replied heatedly. So much for the plan to keep quiet. "In fact, everyone who was in the room seems to agree that it makes you the most likely person to have been behind Art's death." She hazarded a quick glance at the sheriff to see how much trouble she was in, but he continued to stare emotionless at Gabriel Spurlock.

"I was testing him," said Gabriel. "I wanted to see how he acted in an antagonistic atmosphere. I was just pushing the buttons that I thought would make him upset."

"Why?"

"Because, if I'm going to go into business with someone, I need to know what they're like. It's no good knowing what people are like in a comfortable setting. You need to know how they react in less-than-ideal situations."

Eve thought she had pushed the boundaries of interview-interrupting to the limit and thought she should now be quiet—for real this time. After a few beats of silence, during which Eve was congratulating herself on keeping her mouth shut, the sheriff spoke up and said, "Okay. So, how did you feel about his reaction?"

"Favorably," Gabriel answered. "He stood his ground, showed his teeth, argued his point and didn't get overly emotional. I decided I could do business with him, if he had been agreeable, that is. But I never got the chance to broach the subject so, it doesn't matter now. I'm out. I certainly can't do business with her."

"Her?"

"His intellectual property doesn't just vanish. It will be inherited."

"By Mrs. Wells, you mean?"

"Oh. I suppose that's a possibility. But I assumed that his work endeavors would go to his partner in work, not his partner in life. Or in the case of Arthur and Margo Wells, his partner in unhappiness. But if that's the case… Hmmm." Gabriel briefly paused as he stroked his beard. "But… no, I doubt it. I am fairly certain that Art's work is to be inherited by Dr. Hudson. And I certainly cannot work with that woman. There is something about Olive Hudson that I do not trust."

\*\*\*

When the sheriff had made it clear that the interview with Gabriel was finished, Eve stood to open the door for him. She wasn't sure that the sheriff appreciated her gestures of hospitality during official police interviews, but she couldn't help it. She couldn't turn off her hostess skills.

As she opened the door she saw a flash of purple. Instead of letting Gabriel leave, she jumped in front of him so that she could stick her head out of the door jamb to investigate. As she suspected, the purple belonged to Lorenzo's snug fitting shirt. She watched him as he walked to the front of the hotel lobby. No one else was in the room. She wondered if he had been listening at the door to hear Gabriel's interview. She was pretty sure he had been. Otherwise, why would he be walking towards the front door if not to disguise his previous location in front of the office door? She continued to watch Lorenzo as he opened the front door and walk out. She assumed he had no other option if he was going to pretend to be going somewhere.

She turned back to find Gabriel's scowl had returned and was again directed at her.

"Sorry," she said as she stepped out of his way.

She was not surprised that after closing the door the sheriff said, "You know, you don't have to be so nice to these people."

"That's not true," she responded. "YOU don't have to be nice to them. I do. These are my guests. Sure, one of them doesn't deserve my hospitality but everyone else— everyone who didn't kill Art— does deserve it. They are not only my guests but they are having one of the worst days of their lives. I don't want it to be one of the worst hotels stays of their lives on top of that. The world runs on ratings these days. I don't want my reviews to read 'One star. Relentlessly accused of murder.' I want them to read 'Four stars. Pleasantly accused of murder.'"

Sheriff Strider laughed. "Is this out of five stars?"

"Yes," Eve replied with mock seriousness. "You have to expect to lose a star with a murder stay."

"What were you looking at in the lobby?"

"Lorenzo was walking out the front door."

Sheriff Strider's smile vanished. "Good show, was it?"

Eve couldn't help herself. She smiled broadly for a few beats while she tried to think of how to respond to his jealous comment. In the end, she decided to not acknowledge it. Proud of her mature resolve, she simply said, "I think he was eavesdropping at the door and was scurrying off."

"At this door?"

"Yes."

"But you don't know for sure?"

"No, and there wasn't anyone else in the room for me to ask."

"Hmph. We'll have to keep our eyes on him."

Eve's recent maturity vanished. She knew she shouldn't, but she did. She smiled and said, "Don't mind if I do!"

Sheriff Strider's scowl put Gabriel's to shame.

## Chapter Sixteen

Eve wasn't quite sure how she had got there, but she was once again on the couch with Reid. She remembered vaguely that he had asked her to sit and she had complied. There was something about the twinkle in his eye and the smoothness of his voice that was hard to deny. Eve had come to the conclusion that his powers of persuasion worked as well on humans as they did on horses. It solidified her thought that horses were people too. And they were all easily charmed by Reid Tolliver. Of course, Reid had come to Eve's aid during a particularly difficult time and she also felt she owed him. If he wanted her to sit down and be charmed, who was she to say no?

"Hey," said a voice from behind.

Eve drew her attention away from her couch companion and turned to find Naiya and Burt.

"Can I talk to you for a minute?" Naiya asked Eve. "Privately?"

Eve jumped up, easily redirecting her focus to her friend. "Sure," she said as she waved to Naiya to follow her into the manager's suite.

After closing the door behind her, Naiya said, "I wanted to ask you something."

"Something sensitive?" Eve asked with concern, looking at the closed door.

Naiya chuckled as she sat on the love seat. "No. I just wanted an excuse to get away from Burt. I needed a break from him watching over me like I'm a wounded bird."

"He's just being nice."

"I know. At least, I think he's being nice. It's impossible to completely trust anyone here right now."

"Except me, right?"

"Eh," Naiya grunted with a comical shrug of her shoulders. "Although you seem to be fine with trusting Reid."

"Are you jealous? Do you need attention my wounded bird?"

"No. I'm just making sure that you and Reid don't get married because I swear, if he moves here and you bring in a third veterinarian to live in Juniper County I will lose it. Lose it!"

"Okay, okay," Eve said with hands in the air. "I'll pump the breaks on the marriage proposal I was planning," she added sarcastically. "Hey, where are the dogs?" she asked as she looked around the small apartment.

"Ramon took them out for a walk. Well, I think Ramon is just standing in the rose garden while he watches the dogs run back and forth and play in the snow."

"Any chance the snow is melting?"

"Not enough for anyone to leave, not that we're allowed to. I think it melted a little bit but it's getting colder again which means the little bit that did melt will just make the roads even icier. It's dangerous just to go out on the front porch."

"Oh, I should put some salt out there."

"Ramon already did."

"Of course he did," Eve said happily. "I have such a

great staff."

"I used to have a good staff," Naiya said sadly.

"Still bummed about Cheryl leaving?"

"Yes. Can I poach one of your employees?"

"You know I love you like a sister but employee poaching in a rural area... that's just as bad as cattle rustling or horse thievery. Don't you know that employee thieves will be shot on site? Don't make me go from loving you like a fake sister to loving you like a real sister."

"What do you know? You don't have a real sister."

"I've heard things."

"You better watch it — sister," Naiya added pointedly. "Roxie loves me. She might want to come work for me on her own volition."

Eve smiled contentedly. She was happy to see that Naiya was getting back to her snarky, silly self. "What did you want to ask me?"

"Well, speaking of Roxie loving me... Emily created a pub trivia event for all the hotel guests to play. Tonight was supposed to be the night we had it."

"Yes, I remember. Roxie was so looking forward to moderating that. I thought it was strange that you agreed to let her do it. I kind of thought I was the obvious candidate for the job," Eve added with a melodramatic pout.

"I was going to ask you to moderate the trivia night, but Roxie heard about it and begged me to do it. She's so entertaining and adorable. I thought everyone would get a kick out of her. And she's taken the responsibility very seriously. She's been practicing the questions and her presentation for days."

"She must be sad that it's not happening."

"Well, that's the thing — now she's begging me to still do it."

Eve gently shook her head in a way that she had adopted when thinking of Roxie's ridiculousness. "No one is going to want to do that!"

"Well, that's the other thing— they do. Some people were complaining about being bored and Roxie suggested we do the pub trivia this afternoon. Everyone seems agreeable."

"Even grumpy Gabriel?"

"Yes," Naiya said with a laugh. "He said if afternoon pub trivia meant that he would have an excuse to start drinking early, he was in."

"Okay, so are you just asking me for my permission?"

"Well, I thought it would be good to get Sheriff Strider's approval so we don't get in the way of his investigation. So, if you could grease those wheels, that would be great. But also, I need someone to take Art's spot."

"Oh."

"I thought it might be nice to get our minds off of him for a little bit but his absence will be noticeable if we have a team missing a person. I asked Margo if she'd like to join, just to be inclusive, but I'm happy to report that she declined."

"I hope she didn't use grieving the death of her husband as her excuse."

"No. She cited 'not having time for anything so idiotic.'"

Eve agreed to see if she could get the sheriff on board with the trivia event and she set out on her mission. She crossed the lobby quickly as a preventative measure to not get lured back onto the couch with Reid. The office door was open, and Ramon was in the office talking to the sheriff. They abruptly stopped their conversation when Eve appeared, and Ramon made an excuse to leave.

Eve closed the door and got straight to the point. "Will you do me a favor?"

"Are you under the impression that I'm capable of saying no to you?" said Sheriff Strider as his cheekbones raised just enough to make eyes smile.

"What if I asked you to do something outrageous?"

"You wouldn't."

"You're right. I wouldn't. I'm only asking for a pub trivia afternoon."

"Uh… Are you… What?" he asked, looking at her with mild confusion. "I'm going to need more information."

"Why?" she asked with a smile. "Didn't you already say you were incapable of saying no to me?"

"I'd still like to know what I'm getting myself into."

"That's fair," she said. She explained the proposed event. "I think it might be a good idea to get everyone together in a comfortable atmosphere. They might get talkative and say something useful."

"Not if I'm around," the sheriff pointed out.

"No, not if you're around," she agreed. "I was thinking you could sit this one out and let me take over."

"You think that they'll open up around you? You've been in a lot of their interviews with me and have asked questions in those interviews."

"Yes, but I'm not threatening."

He raised his eyebrows. "You're not?"

"I'm too adorable to be taken seriously."

"I want to argue that point, but I feel like any stance I take is going to be considered insulting somehow."

"You are a wise man."

"Fine. I'll hide in here. I need to check in with the deputies and make a few inquiries anyway. You can be my eyes and ears during trivia, but you have to report back to me."

"Okay." A tiredness washed over Eve. She thought about how fun it would be to play a game of carefree trivia without having to suspect all the players of murder. She was ready for this investigation to be behind them. "So… since you are so amenable to my suggestions at the moment, go ahead and just arrest Margo."

"Well, look at that. You proved me wrong. I am

capable of saying no to you. NO."

"Why not?" whined Eve. "She's so horrible and is probably guilty."

"Why don't I arrest Dr. Tolliver?" asked the sheriff.

"Why would you do that?"

"Because I'd like to. But I won't because I don't arrest a person based on the fact that I don't like them. I arrest them because I have proof that they did something illegal."

"But Margo did it. Everyone thinks so."

"Get me evidence and I'll arrest her."

"Maybe I will," Eve said childishly.

"Fantastic. Maybe she'll confess during trivia. Is that what you think is going to happen? I've never played. Is that a thing that normally happens during trivia? People confess their deepest darkest secrets?"

"She's not playing," Eve admitted.

"Oh really?"

"In fact, she's the only one not playing," she added sheepishly.

"So…" Sheriff Strider drew out the word as judgmentally as possible before adding, "you want to hold a trivia event to ferret out the murderer, except the person you think is the murderer won't even be there."

"I'm keeping an open mind."

"I think you just want to play trivia."

In response, Eve shrugged her shoulders and smiled precociously before walking out of the office.

# Chapter Seventeen

Preparations for afternoon pub trivia were in full swing. Chicken nachos had been chosen as the trivia meal, so when Eve entered the kitchen she wasn't surprised to find Ramon at the counter seasoning a large bowl of shredded chicken. On the counter, next to the large bowl was a small bowl of unseasoned chicken.

"What is this bowl of plain chicken for?" Eve asked.

"Oh," said Ramon, "That's Esperanza's sacrifice to the dogs."

"Sacrifice to the gods?"

"No, sacrifice to the dogs. Sunset and Midas. Every time she makes chicken, she keeps a little plain chicken set aside for Sunset. And now that he has a guest, she wants to make sure that they both get a special treat along with the humans.

The walk-in refrigerator door opened and Esperanza stepped into the room.

"I've been wondering why my dog loves you more than me," Eve said to her. "Now I know. Chicken bribing."

Esperanza giggled. "I work with what I have."

Ramon nodded his head as he folded the seasoning into the chicken. "Times may change, but blackmailing and bribing will never go out of fashion."

"What is it?" Esperanza asked in response to Eve's furrowed brow.

"Oh, I don't know," Eve replied, "I just had a thought, or almost had a thought. It's gone now. I guess that's my big accomplishment for today. I ALMOST had a thought."

Esperanza laughed. Eve looked appreciatively at the hotel's cook/mother figure. Esperanza's smile filled any room with comfort and warmth. Eve let herself take a moment to soak it up. Earlier, Eve had spoken privately with Ramon and Esperanza about Art's untimely demise. Eve knew that Esperanza was able to keep in high spirits because she was holding out hope that Art's death was a tragic accident. Eve didn't want to disabuse her of the notion. Esperanza was such a loving, sensitive soul. Eve wanted her to stay that way for today and forever. Plus, keeping a smile on Esperanza's face was beneficial to Eve. It was like a tonic that washed away the evils of the world, if only for a few minutes.

The kitchen's external door opened, and Loretta walked in, bringing a blast of icy cold air with her.

"What were you doing out there?" Eve asked.

Loretta held up the phone in her hand. "Taking a picture of the path I had to shovel to the laundry room."

"Why?"

"'Cause Bridget don't believe me when I tell her that we're snowed in."

"She chose her vacation time more wisely than she realized," said Ramon.

"Ain't that the truth!" agreed Loretta while she fiddled with her phone. "Look at the picture she sent me." She held it up for them to see an image of Bridget basking in the sunshine on the shore of a beautiful blue lake with a cocktail in her hand.

"I wish I was there with her," said Eve.

"Oh, who needs that when we have pub trivia and chicken nachos," said Ramon with his sunny disposition that Eve relied on as much as she did Esperanza's comforting smile.

"I wish you could be on my team Ramon," Eve said wistfully. "You know everything."

"Don't you dare tell my husband he knows everything," laughed Esperanza. "My job is to make him believe that I am the one who knows everything."

Ramon obediently nodded. "Yes, you do, dear. You do."

"Esperanza, you might know all the important things, but Ramon knows all the trivial things," Eve suggested. "And that's what trivia is about."

"I will admit to that," said Esperanza. "And, of course, you know I'm joking. My Ramon does know everything and if he doesn't, he learns how. Just look at how he figured out that microphone system for Dr. Nadar. I can't believe how tiny they can make those wireless microphones these days. All this modern technology blows my mind! I miss the old-fashioned microphones that you held in your hand. Do they have those anymore?"

"Yes, they are still around, my love," Ramon said to his wife. "Just like you and me, handheld microphones are classics. Yes, there are plenty of newer, smaller models on the market, but people still appreciate the sturdiness and reliability of a well-made old-fashioned microphone."

"Yeah," said Loretta, "isn't Roxanne gonna use one of those for trivia? She's been practicing with a hairbrush."

"Yes, she is," Ramon replied to Loretta. To Esperanza, he said, "See darling, classics stand the test of time."

With her delightful smile and a laugh in her melodic voice, Esperanza said, "Oh, don't you try and gloss over the fact that you just called me sturdy and well-made.

Anyway, what I was saying was... What was I saying? See, Eve, you're not the only one who loses their thoughts. Oh yes, my point is—I'm sure my wonderful husband would excel at trivia, just like he does everything else, you know, like setting up microphones— which is where I lost my thought. Anyway, he would be a trivia ringer. We'll have to have an employee trivia night sometime."

"Yeah, that'd be fun," said Loretta. "But Roxanne ain't going to run that one!"

Eve promised to organize an employee trivia night in the near future and asked if she could help them prepare. She was politely told that her services were unneeded in the kitchen. She thanked them, as she always did, and left through the swinging exit door to the lobby. As she walked toward the dining room, she tried to regain the thought she almost had. She felt like she had almost made a connection of some sort. Or at least had a thought that could have been a connection, but it was eluding her. When she got to the dining room she was surprised to see that the majority of the hotel guests were already in there, waiting for the trivia event to begin. She had assumed that Roxie's insistence that people wanted to play was more fiction than truth. She thought that Roxie had coaxed them into agreeing. But looking around the room, Eve got the impression that everyone was eager for a way to pass the time. Eve understood the feeling. Being snowed in after a dreadful tragedy was somehow casting both an air of anxiety and monotony.

Roxie was running around getting people drinks. Eve was happy to jump in and help. She took over drink orders and let Roxie take her place at the podium in front of the four tables that had been arranged for the contest.

As Eve supplied drinks, she couldn't help but notice Olive sitting in the corner, furtively watching everyone else in the room over the top of an open book that she obviously wasn't reading. At that moment, she understood why Gabriel Spurlock might find Olive untrustworthy. As Roxie would say, Olive looked *hella* suspicious.

Colin and Jessica walked in together right behind Loretta who had come in and insisted that she take over as drinks waitress and told Eve to relax. Eve thanked her but knew that relaxing wasn't an option. She was supposed to be working on behalf of the sheriff, trying to suss out information. She stood by the bar and took a visual inventory of everyone present. The only person missing in the dining room was Reid. No sooner had she thought of him, than he appeared. He caught her eye and began to make his way over to her when he was stopped by a wall of sound.

"Okay!" Roxie's voice echoed through the room as she yelled into a microphone. "Looks like everyone is here!"

Naiya stood and whispered something to Roxie. When Roxie continued speaking it was at a reasonable decibel level. Eve realized that Naiya must have explained to Roxie that you either project your voice or you use a microphone, you don't do both. Practicing with a hairbrush could only prepare her for so much.

Reid removed his hands from the sides of his head where he had instinctually put them to protect his eardrums and once again began walking towards Eve. "Hello, I—"

"Okay! Time to get into teams!" Roxie said into her microphone, still loud enough to stop every conversation in the room. Eve had to give it to Roxie. She was successfully using her position as MC to command attention. "At this table, we have team number one: Reid, Sheila, and Lorenzo."

Reid flashed Eve a cute smile and shrugged his shoulders before he walked over to the other side of the room as directed. Olive had been sitting at that table and was forced to close her book/shield and stand up to move. Sheila, overjoyed at her placement, silently clapped her hands as she joined Lorenzo and Reid at table one on the east side of the room.

"Okay!" Roxie continued. "Team number two is here," she said as she pointed to the next table. "Olive, Colin, and Henry." As Olive was standing next to the empty table, she was first to choose a seat. She looked around as if to see which seat might give her the best vantage of the room. As Colin and Henry approached and her time was running out she chose the middle seat. Eve thought that's what she would do. Just like Eve, Olive was in investigation mode and that way she was guaranteed to sit next to Colin. After all, Henry wasn't on the suspect list since he had an air-tight alibi. Henry and Colin set down their beers and sat themselves on either side of Olive.

"Ah!" Kelly said with theatrical disappointment. "I wanted to be on Henry's team!"

"Sorry," said Roxie. "These are the teams. Team three at this table, Kelly, Naiya, and Gabriel."

As Kelly and Naiya were already sitting at the table, Kelly laughed and said, "Well, at least we don't have to get up!"

Gabriel, wearing a more pleasant expression than usual, joined them at table three with his glass of scotch on the rocks.

"And last but not least, team four! Jessica, Burt, and Eve," Roxie announced as she pointed to the table on the west side of the room.

Eve was standing next to the table and quickly secured her preferred seat. It was the one with the best view to look out over the rest of the room. *Eat your heart out, Olive.* She didn't know what she might see that would be of interest but she had promised the sheriff that she would report back. At least in this position she could keep an eye on everyone.

"And now, the fun part!" said Roxie. "Come up with your team name!"

The chair on the opposite side of the table screeched

as Burt pulled it out to sit. For a moment, Eve wondered if he purposefully didn't want to sit next to her. Then, when she realized that his chair choice put him in close proximity to Naiya, she wondered if that had been the deciding factor. Jessica quietly pulled out her chair and sat in the middle of Burt and Eve as she carefully placed her Tom Collins on a cocktail napkin. Eve noticed how graceful Jessica's movements were.

"Are you a ballet dancer?" Eve asked.

Jessica smiled pleasantly. "Why do you ask? Is it the bun?"

"You are so poised and have such great posture," said Eve. "I feel like a clumsy ox around you."

Jessica laughed. "I was forced to take ballet as a child. I never liked it, but that kind of training, or childhood trauma as I think of it, shapes you whether you like it or not."

"Was it really that bad?" Eve asked. "Looking back, I wish I would have been able to take ballet, but we didn't have money for things like that."

"Consider yourself lucky. My ballet instructor, Mistress Peach, was not a peach, she was a tyrant. I learned how to hold myself, but I learned how to hate myself. I learned how to tiptoe through a room without making a sound, but I wanted to use that skill to sneak up behind Mistress Peach and throttle her." Jessica laughed and took a sip of her cocktail. "Like I said, consider yourself lucky. I would have loved to have been a kid who was allowed to be a clumsy ox."

"Not having enough structure as a child can be just as bad," said Burt. "I was practically feral. I was far too used to doing anything I wanted."

"Okay! Let's go backwards. Team four, what is your team name?" Roxie asked Eve's table.

"Already?" Eve asked, looking at her teammates guiltily for not following instructions.

"The Clumsy Oxen!" said Burt with a laugh.

"Yes!" Jessica agreed. "I love it!"

"Weird," said Roxie. "But okay, I guess. The Clumsy Oxygen," she said as she wrote it down on her paper at the podium.

"Oxen," Gabriel corrected her. "O-X-E-N. It's the plural for ox."

Roxie fixed her paper as she said. "Okay. No less weird though. The Clumsy Oxen. Okay! Table three. What is your team name?"

Gabriel shook his head disapprovingly but said, "Go ahead," to his teammates.

"Let's Get Quizzical!" Kelly called out.

The crowd chuckled. Henry said loudly, "Kelly! Are you drunk already?" which received more chuckles.

Olive was laughing the loudest. She said, "Gabriel, you approved of that name?"

"Certainly not," replied Gabriel, "but I was outvoted. It's a good thing I'm not in politics. I refuse to pander to the lowest common denominator and shudder at the decisions made by popular vote."

Gabriel's disapproval only fueled Naiya and Kelly's delight at their chosen name. Eve was so happy to see Naiya with a smile on her face.

"Okay!" Roxie said, quieting the room. "What about table two? What did you come up with for a name?"

"We're Here for the Nachos," said Henry proudly.

Roxie scrunched up her nose. "That's your team name or are you asking for food?"

"Both!" Henry laughed.

"Okay." Roxie wrote down the name. "And table one, what is your team name?"

Sheila nudged Lorenzo. Lorenzo said "Dynamite," and Sheila added, "Because we're going to blow you away!"

"Okay Dynamite, that's a lot to live up to," Roxie said as she wrote down the name.

Loretta was setting down a hot tea in front of Olive

and making a show of rolling her eyes at her daughter's newfound career. But Eve knew that Loretta thought it was as adorable as Eve did. In fact, Eve was trying to not beam with pride at how well Roxie was doing at her trivia moderator gig.

Roxie explained the rules of the trivia game before excitedly announcing, "Okay! First question! What is the term for a horse that has not won a race at a recognized racetrack?"

"Of course, horse racing right out of the gate," said Jessica with a venomous tone that stopped Eve from commenting on the pun in her statement.

"I believe the term is 'maiden'," said Burt.

"Yes, it is," said Jessica. "A sexist term for an evil sport. Horse racing should be outlawed."

"I agree that its regulations and monitoring could use improvement," said Burt. "A lot of improvement," he added.

"No. Outlawed," Jessica insisted. "It's no better than cock fighting. It's abusive and self-serving. As veterinarians, we need to be the champions of animals. We need to speak for those who can't."

"I admire your passion, and I agree that we need to be the ones looking out for horses. I most certainly agree."

Jessica nodded, accepting his response. Eve thought Burt's response was very skilled. He both placated Jessica and didn't lie. He simply agreed with the part of her manifesto that he believed. *Burt may look rough*, Eve thought, *but he is smooth.*

## Chapter Eighteen

Eve kept her eyes on everyone during trivia as best she could without it being too noticeable to her teammates. Not that there was much to see.

As Eve suspected, Olive kept talking to Colin and ignoring Henry. When Colin ordered another beer, Olive commented that he needn't lean so heavily on the 'pub' part of pub trivia. He jovially replied, "Sobriety doesn't suit me. At least, not at times like these."

The only other thing Eve found of interest was Sheila's pouting. Lorenzo and Reid kept chatting, leaving Sheila out of the conversation. Sheila was obviously disappointed with her unexpected role as third wheel.

Soon the anticipated nachos were delivered along with another round of drinks. After a few more questions, noshing on nachos, and yet another beer for Colin, he requested a break. Some of the other contestants, who were also drinking more than their bladders allowed, seconded the motion.

Eve used the time during the break to apologize to her teammates for being the lame wheel. She hadn't been very helpful as the trivia questions had been directed to the skillset of veterinarians, not hotel owners.

"Oh, it's fine," Burt responded. "I'm just glad Margo's not here," he added.

"Me too," agreed Jessica.

"Do you know her from back home?" Eve asked Jessica.

"Uh, no, not really," Jessica replied with discomfort. "She's just been so unpleasant the last few days. I'm sure everyone is happy she's not here. I need to use the ladies' room. Excuse me." Jessica gracefully departed.

"Do you know Jessica from back home?" Eve asked Burt, trying to impart a tone of conversation rather than interrogation.

"No. Never met her."

"She was at the CARED fundraiser."

"As a volunteer?"

"No. She was there as a guest."

His forehead wrinkled. "A guest?"

"Yes."

"Hmmm. There were a lot of guests and I didn't talk to any of them. I'm a backstage kind of guy."

"To be honest," said Eve conspiratorially, "I'm also glad Margo isn't here. I'm having much more fun playing trivia without having to pretend to be nice to the woman who probably killed her husband yesterday."

Burt gave her a guilty look.

"What?" asked Eve in a hushed but imposing tone to impart her insistence on an explanation.

After leaning in as close as he could from across the table, Burt whispered, "Remember when I was talking to the sheriff and I said I didn't see anything strange around the time Art was killed?"

"Yes."

"I lied, I guess. I did see something strange," said Burt apologetically.

"What?"

"Margo. She had a sinful smile on her face. You know,

when I saw her on her balcony."

"That's all?"

"Yes. That's all. That's why I didn't say anything. It sounded stupid and accusatory, and kind of made up, but it's not. It was suspicious. But even though I do agree with you and I think she is the one responsible for my friend's death, a nasty smile on the face of a nasty woman is not proof of anything. I felt like if I told you, it would sound, oh, I don't know, like I was trying to deflect attention from myself. It sounds stupid but I swear she looked like she was up to something."

Eve's earlier elusive thought started to once again tickle at her brain. It was something about Margo… Yes! That was it! Margo. Blackmail. Was Margo blackmailing someone? It had been bothering Eve that everyone insisted Art and Margo had very little money and yet Margo was so well dressed, wearing $1200 shoes, and carrying a expensive limited-edition purse. And when Art and Margo arrived at the hotel, they pulled up in one of the biggest, fanciest, SUV rentals you could get. Something that Margo probably insisted on. But how could she afford these extravagances if they didn't have any money? Margo was obviously getting money from somewhere.

Throughout the rest of trivia, Eve tried to play while simultaneously looking and listening for anything that might be of interest to report back to the sheriff. The only thing she found interesting was a conversation she overheard Olive having with Henry, who had finally weaseled his way into the conversation of his teammates. Art wasn't just a vet, Olive was saying, he was a scientist like her. They got along great, always trying to make improvements to the veterinary field. They trusted each other even if they didn't share every little detail of their lives. She didn't say it outright, but during the short conversation, Eve got the impression that Olive was alluding to the fact that the veterinary practice and all of

Art's work matters would be inherited by her.

Eve became self-conscious of her eavesdropping when she realized that Burt was looking at her curiously. Eve smiled at him as innocently as she could.

"And our final question!" Roxie announced. "What is the name of a zebra donkey hybrid?"

The teams put their heads together and quietly conferred. Eve's team was at a loss.

"Is that real?" Eve asked. "I feel so bad. These questions have all been about animals and since I'm not a veterinarian, I don't know anything. Sorry for being the dead weight."

"Don't be sorry," said Burt kindly. "I'm a vet and I've met a lot of donkeys, but I've never met a zebra, so I don't know the answer either."

"You don't run in zebra circles?" Eve joked.

Burt shook his head and smiled.

Jessica said, "I've known people who had zebras but why on earth would anyone breed them with donkeys?"

"Probably nobody," answered Burt. "I imagine this is only a thing that happens when a zebra and a donkey love each other very, very much."

Eve chuckled as she said, "I'm going to take a wild stab and say zonkey."

Burt nodded. "Sounds good to me."

Jessica also agreed. Eve's team gave their answer of zonkey, Naiya's team said deebra, Olive's team said zeedonk, and Reid's team said zeebrass, which Sheila could not stop giggling over.

"Okay! So, the winner of the last question is... EVERYONE! Those are all right answers. A zebra donkey can be called any of those and can also be called a zebronkey or zebadonk."

"Hey!" Eve said to her teammates. "I guess sometimes a wild stab at the answer works."

"Okay!" said Roxie, who hadn't lost any of her enthusiasm or energy, unlike most of the contestants. The day drinking had created an epidemic of yawning. "Our totals are…" Roxie continued with vigor, "the Clumsy Oxen in last place with 15 points. We're Here for the Nachos in third place with 18 points. Dynamite blew ALMOST everyone away with 20 points. And congratulations to the winners, Let's Get Quizzical, with 22 points!" Roxie started a round of applause for the winners.

"What do we win?" Kelly asked as she attempted to stifle a yawn.

"We get to go take a nap," said Naiya.

"Oh good, that's what I wanted to win," laughed Kelly.

"I would have preferred a cash prize," said Gabriel. "But a nap will do. Along with the satisfaction that we're better than everyone, of course."

Everyone stood, stretched, finished drinks, and gathered their things.

"Thank you, my fellow Clumsy Oxen, for being my teammates," Eve said to Jessica and Burt. I know we lost but I still had fun."

"Me too," said Burt. "It was nice to take my mind off of things for a while."

"Honestly, I'm happy to be here," Jessica said. "I know the circumstances aren't ideal but this is kind of a vacation for me. Back home my schedule is very rigid."

"Don't tell me that your parents are still making you take ballet lessons," Burt joked.

"My parents died when I was twenty," Jessica said, emotionless, as if commenting on the weather.

"Oh," Eve blurted out, thinking that was such a strange response. She assumed Jessica wanted to talk about it since she brought it up, so she asked, "How did your parents die?"

"Barn fire."

"I'm so sorry for your loss," Burt said uncomfortably.

"Don't be," Jessica said with continued detachment.

"It wasn't much of a loss. Well, I shouldn't say that. It was a great barn." Jessica quietly and gracefully walked into the lobby leaving Eve and Burt to share a look of concern.

*** 

After trivia, everyone unapologetically retired to their rooms.

Eve watched Naiya with jealousy as she walked to their shared suite to lie down and snuggle the dogs. Eve couldn't join her. She had a debriefing to attend to. Her own moderate day drinking cause her to giggle internally at the word "debrief" as she knocked on the office door. She listened for a "Come in" but the door opened, and the sheriff waved her in with a "Welcome" instead.

"I remember when this was my office," Eve said as she sauntered by him with a smile.

"Ah, the good old days. I remember those. Oh well, mine now. Did you learn anything?"

"Trivia-wise or deep-dark-secret-wise?"

"Dealer's choice."

"I learned that great white sharks have up to seven rows of teeth."

"Interesting. Anything else?"

"Jessica might have seven rows of teeth."

"Even more interesting. Please elaborate."

"I don't know, I like her and then I think I shouldn't. Then I like her again and she says something odd and sometimes disturbing. I can't tell if she's eccentric, fun, deranged, sweet, or a murderer. She's thrown me for a loop." Eve proceeded to tell the sheriff all the information she learned and behavior she found interesting. After summing it all up, it didn't amount to much. It was an underwhelming debriefing. The sheriff got a call and she used the opportunity to leave to go see Naiya and the dogs.

Naiya was lying on the bed reading a book. The dogs

were in their dog beds. Eve laughed. Usually, Sunset insisted on being on the human bed. She wondered if he was pretending to be a good boy for Midas's sake or for Naiya's.

Eve lay down on the bed and got out her phone to see if she had received any texts from Wes. She hadn't. There was only a new text from her mother. She knew she shouldn't worry. Wes was busy. Eve distracted herself by reading the long text from her mother and sending an equally long response.

"What's that noise?" asked Naiya.

"What noise?" asked Eve.

"Listen," she said huffily.

Eve concentrated listening for a strange noise. She finally heard the faint buzz. It sounded familiar but she couldn't place it. "I'd say it was the flight school landing a plane out at the airstrip, but that can't be it. They wouldn't be attempting that in the snow."

"A blender?" Naiya suggested.

"Oh, you're probably right," Eve said. She shook her head. "I wouldn't put it past Roxie to be making another milkshake."

"That's probably it," said Naiya as she set down her book and closed her eyes. "That's the most likely answer."

Eve thought about those words "the most likely answer" as she set down her phone on the nightstand. The most likely answer... Margo was the most likely answer. Eve needed to focus on proving Margo's guilt because Margo was the most likely answer. Eve was hoping that she would have a revelation on how she could prove Margo was the murderer, but that did not happen. Her thoughts only continued to swirl around her head until they began mixing with her subconscious and the jumbled mess of ideas lured her to sleep.

## Chapter Nineteen

Naiya was still asleep when Eve woke up from her nap. She was groggy and disappointed in herself for allowing herself to fall asleep.

When she quietly closed the door behind her and entered the lobby, she found Lorenzo and Olive talking quietly on the couch. They stopped talking and looked up as soon as they realized they weren't alone. Eve smiled and nodded on her way to the bar in the dining room. On the very rare occasion she took a nap, she craved a sugary beverage afterwards. She would treat herself to a rare soda after her rare nap. She made her way to the dining room, still a little unsteady as she tried to shake off the effects of the nap. Upon entering the empty dining room, she was taken aback when the back door opened and Loretta rushed in.

"What are you doing?" Eve asked, calming herself after the minor fright. At least she wasn't groggy anymore.

"I was sweeping the snow off the veranda," Loretta replied. "And then I seen footprints in the snow!" she whispered excitedly. "You wasn't out there, was you?"

"No," Eve replied at regular volume. "They're Colin and Lorenzo's footprints. They're helping look after the horses. I thought I told you that."

"No! Not footprints to the stables. Footprints out to the driveway, heading back, like towards the cabins."

"What? Who would be walking out there?"

"I don't know but I thought I should tell you."

"Okay, thanks. I'll let the sheriff know."

Eve grabbed her soda from the bar's refrigerator. By the time she walked back through the lobby, both Olive and Lorenzo had disappeared. She went to the office but found it empty. She went to the kitchen to ask Esperanza if she knew where the sheriff was but didn't need to. He was sitting at the kitchen counter having a sandwich and talking to Ramon, Esperanza, and Roxie.

As she suspected, the suspicious footprints also piqued the sheriff's interest. She talked him into a joint fieldtrip to see where they led. They first stopped in the basement to put on rubber boots. Eve had a variety of sizes down there for the staff to use when it was snowy, rainy, or muddy. Being in dry Arizona, they didn't get used all that often but it was nice to have when you needed them. She also grabbed some underused parkas that were stored down there. Eve liked to be prepared, and the basement afforded her the space to keep numerous 'just in case' supplies. She had never been a cookie-selling girl scout, but she felt like she was a pretty successful always-prepared woman scout.

Unfortunately, by the time they were ready, most everyone had woken from their afternoon naps and were milling about the hotel. All geared-up, Sheriff Strider and Eve attempted to nonchalantly walk through the lobby and dining room wearing their big black rubber boots and fur lined hooded coats. Then they exited out the back door as if they were going for a nice stroll. Eve didn't think that they fooled anyone. After they had made it about a hundred feet from the hotel, she looked back. It was the middle of the day but the clouds were still thick and threatening to unleash even more snow. The sun was barely able to penetrate the cloud cover leaving the world much darker than normal. The dimness allowed Eve to easily see into the brightly lit dining room floor to ceiling windows. Inside was a crowd curiously watching them on their outdoor excursion. Eve turned back to look at the footprints to make out the shape and size of the shoe. "Pointy toes," she said directing the sheriff's attention to the best specimen.

"Looks like cowboy boots," said Sheriff Strider.

"Burt, Colin, and Lorenzo all wear cowboy boots."

"Dr. Spurlock wears pointed wing tips. It could be those also."

"It's definitely not Reid's," said Eve. "His shoes are rounded at the toes."

"You're pretty quick to discount him."

"I'm just pointing out a fact."

"Okay."

"Okay."

They continued to follow the path of footprints, making their own path next to it.

"He might have brought a pointy pair of shoes, that's all I'm saying," said the sheriff.

"Well, I haven't seen him wear any, is all I'm saying."

"You keep notice of his shoes?"

"I am a very observant person."

"Hmmm," Sheriff Strider lightly growled.

"Is there a problem?" Eve asked.

"I think I might be a little jealous."

"Good."

"Good? You think it's good?"

"Actually, I think it's great, but I'm trying to play it cool over here."

"Dr. Tolliver flirts with you a lot."

"Sometimes women like to be flirted with."

"I flirt with you."

Eve literally stopped in her tracks. "You do?"

"Yes."

"Really? Well then, you're not very good at it." She held her breath. Maybe she shouldn't have said that. She thought it was funny, but would he think it was just mean? She was so relieved when he belted out a laugh.

Eve's corresponding smile was short-lived when she realized where the footprints were leading them. It was the tumbleweed pen. Eve stared at the wood slats hiding what was inside. The woodchipper, she reminded herself with a lump in her throat. Without thinking she grabbed onto Sheriff Strider's arm for support. She didn't know if it was only for emotional support or if perhaps her knees had become a little weak.

"What is it?" the sheriff asked worriedly.

"It wasn't a blender."

"What?"

"The noise that Naiya and I heard earlier. It wasn't a blender."

"I don't understand."

Eve pointed to the tumbleweed pen. "It's where we keep the woodchipper for the tumbleweeds."

"That's how you get rid of your tumbleweeds? I don't think that's the best—"

"Not the point," she said with an intense look of uneasiness.

He nodded solemnly and said, "You stay here."

She was so happy he said that. She didn't want to go in. As the sheriff opened the tall wooden gate, Eve stayed behind looking in the opposite direction at the beautiful snow blanketed world. It could have been such a lovely moment but the possibility of horror hung around her like a dirty fog. She looked at the footprints that were not theirs. They had made an effort to not walk in their path. It wasn't obvious, but it looked like the same footprints coming from and going back to the hotel. Eve consoled herself with the fact that she didn't see a second set of footprints going to the pen and not coming back.

"Come in here," said the sheriff's voice behind her, making Eve jump with anxious fear. "Take a look and tell me what you see."

She looked into his eyes as she calmed herself and regulated her breathing. She trusted that if there was something gruesome to see he would have given her a warning. She studied his face. He looked confused more than anything. Her interest was piqued. She walked into the pen and looked at where the sheriff was pointing, at what she called the 'spitter-outer-end' of the woodchipper. Just because she owned a woodchipper didn't mean she knew its anatomy.

"What is that?" asked the sheriff. "It's not tumbleweed pieces."

Eve recognized the cream-colored flakes immediately. "It's my good paper," she said. Someone had used the woodchipper as an emergency paper shredder. "Margo! It has to be Margo. She printed Art's presentations on my good paper. I thought she was faking her limp! Maybe that's why she faked an ankle injury, so that she could come out here and we wouldn't suspect her."

"Those aren't her footprints," the sheriff pointed out. "They're too big."

"Those aren't her shoeprints, you mean," Eve countered. "A small-footed person can always put on a pair of bigger shoes and walk around. In fact, she would probably need to borrow some boots to come out here anyway since she only wears high heels. And apparently those heels are insanely expensive."

"Maybe Art brought some boots with him and she used those," suggested Sheriff Strider. "Did you see him wearing any?"

"No." Eve cocked her head to the side to facilitate more productive thinking. It worked. "Wait. No. That doesn't add up."

"Why?"

"Margo asked to use my paper shredder after she hurt her ankle. I remember her angrily limping off. She couldn't have known that my paper shredder had just broken. She wouldn't have faked an ankle injury to come out here because she would have had no idea that she would have to come up with a different plan that would involve a trek through the snow and operation of a dangerous machine. Plus, I can't see Margo doing this. Burt said that she's the kind of person that treats everyone like they are her servants. I don't see her getting all do-it-yourself with a woodchipper in the snow. But I'm sure that's my good paper and unless someone shred a bunch of my menu inserts, it has to be Art's presentations." Eve took a handful of the paper on the top of the pile that had not yet been wetted by the snow. "For comparison," she said as she put it in her pocket.

"Okay, let's head back," said the sheriff.

"Okay," Eve said but instead of following him as he made his way to the open gate, she closed her eyes and took a deep breath. She exhaled the lingering fear of the possibility of finding something gruesome in the woodchipper pen. And just for good measure, she took another deep breath of the crisp, clean air. Her eyes popped open with sudden realization. The air wasn't clean. Over the smell of the gasoline of the woodchipper was another smell that she recognized. She decided to keep the information to herself for the moment and followed the sheriff out of the pen.

They walked back to the hotel in the same path that they had made next to the shredder's tracks. They walked in a comfortable silence that allowed Eve to take a short mental break. For a few minutes she allowed herself to enjoy the snowy wonderland and the company.

When they returned to the hotel, they ignored the inquisitive stares of the people in the dining room and the lobby as they walked through to the office. She pulled out the two pieces of remaining cream paper, put them on the desk and put the handful of shredded pulp on top of them. It was a perfect match.

"So," began the sheriff slowly as he took off his parka, "now we need to know what was in those presentations that someone was trying to hide."

"That Margo was trying to hide," said Eve. "She's the one who asked to use the paper shredder."

"Does Art have a laptop here with the presentations on them?"

"Margo used a flash drive to print them," said Eve.

"So, we just need to get that flash drive."

"Actually, we don't even need to do that," Eve said with a knowing smile.

"Why?"

"Because, despite the fact that Margo thought my printer was slow, it is brand new and has all the bells and whistles."

"And that means?"

Eve clicked a few buttons on the printer menu. "It means that it has a print history button," she said as the printer whirred to life.

"Neat trick," he said, returning her smug smile.

"That'll teach her to insult my office products," Eve laughed. "They fight back."

As the printer spat out papers they took turns looking at them but realized that they didn't know what they were looking for.

"You know what?" said Eve. "It's probably his last presentation, the secret one. He had the last slot of the conference and it didn't say what it was. It was some sort of big reveal." She grabbed a copy of the conference schedule from her bookshelf. "Look for any title that doesn't match one of Art's listed presentations."

"Here it is," Sheriff Strider said after sifting through the papers again. "It's called 'A New Day for Strength and Endurance.'"

Eve pulled a chair next to his so they could read the

paper together. They sat in silence with their heads together as they focused on reading sheet after sheet of paper. Eve was grateful that the sheriff was not some sort of a speed reader that was always waiting for her to finish the page. They read at the same rate and made it through their shared reading adventure quickly and fluidly. There was a lot of technical information that Eve didn't understand but there was enough for her to get the gist.

When they finished the last page, Eve said, "Wow. That's huge. Right?"

"Yeah," said the sheriff as he looked into her eyes. "Sounds like Dr. Wells thought so."

"Something worth killing for?"

"Definitely. I don't know why someone would kill Dr. Wells over this but it's probably the reason. Well, maybe. It's on the list, on the top of my list at the moment. I need to talk to Mrs. Wells."

## Chapter Twenty

Eve found Margo standing in front of the open door to her downstairs suite, talking with Reid. As she walked up to them, Reid said, "I was just about to bring Margo an iced tea. Would you like anything?"

Eve declined. As Reid walked away, Eve again remembered Burt saying that Margo was the kind of person that treated everyone like they were her servants, and that he was the kind of person that fell for it. Apparently, so was Reid.

Before Margo had the chance to give Eve some sort of order or request, Eve said, "The sheriff wants to talk to you," in her not-polite tone. She had been going for perturbed and possibly even angry, but her inner hotel hostess kicked in and diluted the intended acidity.

"Again?" Margo asked drily.

The fact that Margo was not pitching a fit made Eve suspicious. Eve peeked past the small woman and looked into her room. "I see you haven't unpacked your things."

"The snow will melt soon, and we'll be able to leave. I'm not staying here any longer than I have to."

"It's not just the snow keeping you here, Margo. There is a murder investigation, in case you have forgotten."

"I'm going to leave as soon as I can leave, and I want

to be ready. Is that a crime?"

Reid returned, handed Margo a glass of iced tea, politely smiled at both of them, and walked away.

Eve continued to look at the still packed suitcases in Margo's suite. "Do you have Art's things?"

"No."

"Not even a pair of his boots?" Eve asked, even though she was fairly certain that Margo hadn't done her own dirty work by trekking out to the wood shredder.

"No, certainly not! Why would I have a pair of his boots?"

"Where are his things?"

"I told your girls that I didn't want them. I think they put his things in the basement. I don't need to be lugging around that stuff. I have no use for it."

Eve's heart broke for Art Wells. How could he have spent his life with this callous woman? What a waste. She was filled with rage and disgust. She took Margo's arm and pulled her into the suite and closed the door behind them. She wanted to talk with Margo privately and she didn't want anyone to witness the way she was going to be talking to her. Eve knew that she was furious when her act of minor violence caused iced tea to slosh out of Margo's glass and Eve didn't apologize or attempt to clean it up. Her inner hotel hostess had vanished.

Margo held the dripping glass away at arm's length as if she expected it to be taken from her. Eve ignored it.

"You really don't care that your husband was murdered, do you?" Eve practically hissed. She never talked to people like this. It felt unnatural for her to be mean, but Margo brought out the worst in her. "You don't care at all. You are the most selfish person I have ever met. You certainly don't seem to care if we find out who did it or why they did it. Which only makes me suspect you even more."

Margo set down her untouched iced tea on the nearby table and picked up a towel to dry her wet hand. She calmly said, "I already told you who did it. It was Colin McCullough. But, because you don't like me, you're not listening to me."

Eve knew that she was supposed to bring Margo back to the office so that the sheriff could interview her in an official capacity, but Eve's animosity was making her irrational and impatient. "I know you shredded Art's presentations."

"I don't know what you're talking about," Margo said while crossing her arms and sticking her chin in the air.

"And I know what they said." Eve stared into the abyss of Margo's soulless eyes. "I have a copy of them in my office."

"No, you don't."

"I read 'A New Day for Strength and Endurance' just a few minutes ago."

Margo's composure disappeared. "How did you get that?" She asked angrily in a hushed voice even though they were in a private room. "That is privileged information. You can't tell anyone about that."

"I didn't sign an NDA," Eve snapped. "Plus, I was under the impression that Olive would be inheriting the rights to his work, not you."

"I was his wife. I should be inheriting everything."

"But you're not. You're not even the beneficiary of his life insurance policy."

"I will be after you arrest Colin."

"Margo, stop." Eve ran her fingers through her hair. This woman infuriated her. She took a deep breath and said, "Why did you shred the papers? Why are you trying to keep Art's new drug a secret? I didn't understand everything in the presentation, but it sounds like Art created a miracle drug that can really help weak, sickly horses. That sounds amazing. Why would you want to not share that with the world?"

Margo stared daggers at Eve but said nothing.

"In his presentation," Eve continued, "he said he was

taking his formula to the FDA's Center for Veterinary Medicine office next week. After years of careful tests, he was finally ready to reveal it to the public."

"But he hadn't revealed it, and you can't. You don't have the formula."

"And you do?"

"Maybe."

"But you wouldn't understand it any more than me. And honestly, I doubt you do have it. Art wouldn't trust you with that. He was a cautious man. And although he obviously felt the need to stay married to you, I very much doubt that he confided in you or trusted you at all."

Margo looked at Eve with the calculating stare of a witch who was deciding whether she was going to boil or bake her captive. "You're right, I don't have the formula. It died with Art."

Eve realized Margo's pause had been used to determine which lie she was going to tell. She didn't know what Margo was playing at but she didn't trust any word out of her mouth. *What is it about this drug that is making her cagey?* Eve stopped and replayed the last sentence of her inner dialogue. *Drug, cagey?* Don't those usually go together? Maybe Art's drug has other applications besides helping horses. Colin's quip about sobriety not suiting him flashed in her head. Lots of people use drugs for all kinds of reasons. Pain management, strength training, recreational hallucinogenic purposes. Eve wondered if this drug would be more lucrative if cultivated as a designer but illegal drug. Perhaps Margo wanted to keep it for herself to hurt humans instead of help horses. Was Margo a drug lord? Was she already selling the drug on the side and making the money to fund her couture wardrobe?

Just a few minutes ago Eve couldn't imagine how a drug that was created for the benefit of horses could be a motive for murder. But now, considering the drug might be used for another purpose, it seemed like the most likely motive for the death of Art Wells. Art certainly would not have stood for his drug, his life's work, being used for nefarious purposes.

"Are we done here?" Margo asked nastily, awakening Eve from her trance-like state.

"Done?" Eve barked. "No. I told you, you have to talk to the sheriff."

"Still?"

"Yes, still! I told the sheriff I would bring you to him in the office. Let's go."

"Fine. I have nothing to hide."

"Oh, that's got to be lie," Eve said as she opened the door. She waved for Margo to exit first and watched Margo limp through the doorway. Eve followed Margo through the lobby where Jessica and Olive were reading separately and Reid and Sheila were chatting together. Eve watched Margo with suspicion as she walked behind her. She didn't mind in the slightest if she appeared to be a prison warden. Her time treating Margo like a valued guest was over. Margo was enemy number one as far as she was concerned.

Eve began analyzing Margo's limp and almost burst out laughing when Jessica said, "Oh, please! We all know that you're faking that limp, Margo."

"Excuse me?" Margo hissed as she turned toward Jessica. "Don't talk to me like you know me."

"I will talk to you anyway that I like," said Jessica, easily matching Margo's fierceness.

"No, you will not! No one is allowed to talk to me like that, especially not some mousey veterinarian at a two-bit conference in the backwoods of nowhere."

"Create. Don't berate," Olive's voiced filled the room. She gained everyone's attention.

"Oh, please," said Margo with an eyeroll.

Olive looked at Eve. "Art used to always say that. 'Create. Don't berate.' I loved that saying. He thought you should spend your time building things, not tearing down others. To contribute to society rather than criticize the people that are making an effort. Unfortunately, too often the most vocal critiques come from those who offer nothing to benefit society."

"I'm sure he had his horrible wife in mind when he came up with that saying," said Jessica.

"I told you to shut your mouth," said Margo.

"All you do is berate people and contribute nothing. You're a leech!"

"You don't know me!"

"I know that you are a horrible person," Jessica spat out.

Margo took a step towards Jessica and stared her down. "You— you prissy little—"

"You are a horrible person," Jessica repeated even more loudly. "HORRIBLE!" With fire in her eyes and in her voice she yelled, "And you're a murderer! You killed your husband! You killed him!" Jessica's voice became even more shrill and frantic as she continued screaming, "You killed him! You killed him!"

Everyone in the room became quiet, staring at Jessica as her chest heaved with the heavy breaths caused by her outburst. In the silence it was very easy to hear Reid say, "That voice. It's you. I can't believe it. It's you." He was staring at Jessica with astonishment. "It's you," he repeated. "Jessie Laberge."

## Chapter Twenty-One

Jessica's screaming had caused the sheriff to appear from the office. He remained in the doorway as he watched the drama unfold.

"I can't believe it!" Reid said again to Jessica. "Jessie Laberge! You've been hiding here in plain sight this whole time!"

"I haven't been hiding," Jessica said, slowing her breathing and making an effort to speak in a calm tone.

"What are you doing here? You're up to something!" said Reid. "Why else would you be here? Why would you be using a different name?"

"I go by Jessica now because I'm an adult. And I changed my last name because I got married. It wasn't a subversive act."

"Little Jessie Laberge?" Margo asked in confusion. "You're little Jessie Laberge?"

"Not that you can tell," said Reid. "She's changed her hair, and well, everything. She's disguised herself because she obviously didn't want us to recognize her."

"That's ridiculous!" Jessica said loudly as she put her hands on her hips.

"Is it?" Margo asked.

"Yes!" replied Jessica confidently. "I wear my hair differently and I dress differently but I am not in a disguise. I wear my hair up because I find it convenient and I wear glasses because I need them. I'm not a teenager anymore. You didn't recognize me because it's been seventeen years since you've seen me and because you both are two of the most self-obsessed people in the world. You don't bother to pay attention to other people."

"Maybe I didn't recognize you because you weren't screaming bloody murder at me," said Reid.

"The day is young," Jessica sneered at him.

"You were such a terror," said Margo.

Jessica's head whipped in Margo's direction. "I still can be, so you might want to watch it."

"I'm not your enemy, Jessie," Margo said calmly. "In fact, I really liked your parents."

"My name is Jessica. And of course you liked my parents. They were horrible people too."

"Jessie!" Margo said as she clutched her hand to her chest.

"Jessica," said Jessica, again correcting Margo while shooting her a look of defiance. "In the short time I had Fearless, I received more love from him than both of my parents combined throughout my whole life. It's no wonder that I grieved his loss the way I did." As Jessica continued talking, she once again began ramping up to a fevered pitch. "You all treated me like I was a monster for having feelings after my horse died. But you were the monsters for not having feelings. YOU WERE THE MONSTERS!" After yelling the last sentence, Jessica once again attempted to calm herself. She stood with a heaving chest while everyone stared silently at her.

From the corner, a clear and rational voice said, "Dr. Denmon, may I see you in the office, please?"

Jessica looked at the sheriff like she was a school child who had just been caught misbehaving by the principal.

She nodded her head with an expression of shame and walked slowly over to him.

Margo looked like the cat that ate the canary. She was quite obviously pleased with the fact that she had avoided her interview with the sheriff by sacrificing Jessica.

Propelled partly by wanting to learn more about Jessica Laberge Denmon and partly by the relief that she always felt getting away from Margo, Eve followed Jessica into the office. The sheriff could always kick her out if she wasn't welcome. But he didn't.

Jessica sat in the chair and immediately said, "Yes, yes. I'm Jessica Laberge. Don't bother asking any questions. I'll tell you everything."

"Thank you," said the sheriff as he leaned back and made himself comfortable.

"I know people don't like hearing about how hard it is to be rich," Jessica began, "but it is. At least, it can be. It was for me when I was growing up. My childhood was hard. I would even go so far to say that I was troubled. Yes, I had anything money could buy but I was miserable. The things that were given to me weren't meant to make me happy. The many things that my parents provided for me were for their benefit, not mine. The best schools, clothes, tutors… these were all provided to make me look good so that they looked good. That's all I was to my parents, a possession. My job wasn't to be happy; it was to be pretty, smart, and talented at everything. If I wasn't perfect at everything, my parents were quick to let me know what a disappointment I was. I was no more to them than one of their racehorses. Except when I proved to be a loser, they couldn't just sell me. And of course, since they were horse people, I was expected to be a good rider, so I was always having riding lessons. I grew very fond of our horses, more so than any of the people in my life. When one of their horses, although bred to be a winner, turned out to be a sickly loser they were quick to try and unload him. But I loved that horse even more because he was an unwanted loser, like I felt I was. I had to beg, but they finally let me keep him as my very own horse. It was amazing. I had never been allowed to have a pet. My parents saw no benefit in it. But finally, with Fearless I had an animal to bond with. He took away most of the darkness I felt in my life. He was my best friend. All the love I had yearned for my whole life, I got from Fearless. We were a team. Fearless was my life.

"Then my parents hired Art and Reid as our veterinarians. They took a special interest in Fearless. I didn't know why and I didn't like it. I didn't like anyone who was associated with my parents, and I certainly didn't trust anyone who was employed by them. When my horse died, I blamed Art and Reid. Everyone thought I was being a foolish temperamental child, but Fearless was fine one day and then he was dead the next. My world ended. I was an unloved emotional child who lost the only thing that brought me joy. I pitched such a fit my parents fired them. It wasn't out of devotion to me, mind you. It was just to shut me up. I had reached an age at which I realized that embarrassing my parents was my only bargaining chip.

"But it never stopped hurting and it never stopped bothering me. To my parents' dismay, I chose to become a veterinarian to help animals due to this devasting event in my life. It was the only way I felt I could heal. And it worked, I eventually forgot about it until a year ago. When I saw Art at that fundraiser, then I saw Reid too, all that pain and confusion and unanswered questions came back to haunt me. I couldn't stop thinking about it. When I heard Art and Reid were both going to be at this conference, I decided to come, to confront them about what happened to Fearless."

"But you didn't get the chance," Eve said sadly.

"I did. I talked to Art the night of the reception before the conference. To my surprise, he approached me, he recognized me. He said he'd always kept tabs on me. He said he had been so proud of me when he heard that I had become a veterinarian. He was very apologetic about Fearless. He told me what happened. We were square. The end. I had no ill feelings towards Arthur Wells when he was killed."

"What happened?" asked the sheriff.

"I thought the consensus was that someone introduced the tumbleweed into the stable and—"

"No, not that. What happened with Fearless?"

"Art confided in me and now that he's no longer here, I feel compelled to keep that story between us."

"Does it have something to do with Margo? Is that why you yelled at her?"

"No. If Margo had anything to do with Fearless's death, I would be more than happy to tell you. I just don't like her. I never have. She used to come around the property when Art was working and chat up my parents. The little I know of Margo is that when it comes to the rich, she easily plays the part of sycophant and when it comes to everyone else, it's disdainful indifference. Margo liked my parents because they had boatloads of money and, like I said, I didn't like people who liked my parents. I never liked Margo and now I think she is the most likely person to have killed Art. Art, who I just forgave after so many years. It makes me sick. Margo makes me sick."

"But you don't think Margo had anything to do with Fearless?"

"No. What happened with my horse seventeen years ago has nothing to do with what happened to your horse yesterday, nothing at all."

## Chapter Twenty-Two

To Margo's dismay, the revelation of Jessica's identity only delayed her interview rather than canceling it. "It is really necessary?" Margo whined.

As Margo pouted in the open doorway of her suite, Eve peered inside at the untouched iced tea still sitting on the table. Eve sighed in irritation and said, "Just because a little spilled out, it doesn't mean it's undrinkable."

"What are you talking about?" said Margo.

"The iced tea," Eve said as she pointed to it.

Margo rolled her eyes. "I don't even like iced tea."

"Then why did you ask Reid to get it for you?" Eve asked with frustration. Everything about Margo irked her. It was as if she thought she was getting points for being contrary. "Let's go. The sheriff doesn't like to be kept waiting."

Eve once again escorted Margo across the lobby to the office but when they arrived Eve did not enter with her. She shut the door with as much gravitas as she could imbue the simple act. Eve wanted Margo to be worried, to be scared. She had suggested to the sheriff that she remain absent from the interview so that Margo would be more intimidated by the officiality. Eve realized her presence in the interview might undermine that. Her unfavorable reaction to every little thing Margo did and said was resulting in useless bickering. She was willing to sit out the interview if it meant that Sheriff Strider could put some fear into Margo. He was a kind and good man, but he could be intimidating when needed.

Kelly, Henry, Reid, and Sheila were in the lobby playing a card game around the coffee table. Colin sat alone at the chess table scrolling through screens on his phone. As Eve made her way across the room to her suite, Reid sneezed loudly. "These darn allergies!" he said as he grabbed a tissue from his pocket.

"Bless you," Shiela said loud enough for the benefit of the cheap seats.

Eve cringed. She hated when someone took that kind phrase and said it in a pompous tone of voice that seemed to admonish everyone else in the room for not being as considerate as themself. Of course, Eve wasn't going to comment on that particular reflection, but she did have another sneeze related observation to share.

"You know," Eve said to the group, "I've always thought it was so strange that we are supposed to bless a sneeze but not a cough. A cough can be indicative of a much more serious problem that might need medical attention. It's the symptom more likely to need a blessing."

"You're right," said Colin. "I've never thought about it like that. But, yes, that doesn't make much sense, does it? A sneeze gets a 'bless you' and a cough gets a 'screw you and get away from me before I catch whatever you have.'"

Eve chose to alter her plans of finding comfort in her apartment. She used Colin's agreement with her as a pretense to sit across the chess table from him. "Do you want to play?" she asked, gesturing to the chess board.

He hesitated for a moment before saying, "Sure. Just let me send off a quick text."

Eve was sitting on the side of the white pieces, so she

moved a pawn while she waited for him.

Colin put away his phone and said, "I'm making arrangements to have my ranch renamed the 'Arthur Wells Horse Sanctuary.'"

"What a wonderful tribute," Eve said with feeling. After the opening moves, Eve broached the subject she had intended to discuss with Colin. Quietly, she said, "So, that was a pretty smart idea to sneak into the animal fundraiser to find people who had the means and desire to help with a horse sanctuary."

"The idea was good, I guess, but the execution didn't really work."

"But you met Art," Eve said as she captured one of Colin's pawns.

"Yeah, I guess." Colin quickly moved another pawn leaving a bishop unprotected.

"And now you have the money you needed, from Art and from Reid," Eve said as she captured the bishop.

"Yeah. That's true."

"How did you get in? To the fundraiser, I mean. Wasn't there a lot of security?"

"Oh," Colin chuckled as he moved his rook. "It wasn't like I was avoiding a room of red laser beams or anything. I just paid someone to let me in a side door."

"Aren't you excited about all the things you can do now?" Eve asked as she captured Colin's poorly placed rook with her queen.

"Yeah, I am," he said as he looked up at her. "It's a dream come true. Maybe it was meant to be. It's strange. You know, Reid Tolliver was one of the people that was on my list to talk to at that fundraiser, but I never got the opportunity. Little did I know that the guy who kicked me out of the fundraiser was his old partner. Who could have guessed that I would become friends with Reid Tolliver's old partner and that would lead to me meeting Reid a year later on the other side of the country and getting him to donate. Isn't that crazy? I guess maybe it really was meant to be."

Eve wondered if Margo was right. Was Colin McCullough a world class conman? Perhaps his sweet-natured fate argument was really hiding a carefully planned long con. Had Reid Tolliver been his mark the whole time? Certainly, Art couldn't have been. He didn't have any money. And yet, Colin was getting the lion's share of his new wealth because of Art's death. Receiving a fortune was a whale of a motive. It would be foolish to dismiss simply because Colin seemed like a nice guy. It could be an act, as could his poor chess skills. Was he purposefully hiding his cleverness with these atrocious decisions in this chess game?

"Can I play winner?" Kelly asked as she walked up to them.

Eve looked up to see that the card game had ended and Henry had disappeared. Sheila had inched over toward Reid on the couch and Kelly had probably felt like a third wheel.

"Sure," Colin replied to Kelly's inquiry.

Eve didn't want to play anymore but didn't see how she could possibly throw the game to avoid playing Kelly. She was only two moves away from checkmate. She leaned into it and quickly put Colin out of his misery.

As Kelly sat down to take his place and Eve set up the chess board to start again, she hoped that Kelly was either as bad as Colin or much better than Eve so that the game would be a fast one. Unfortunately, as they got into the match, it was evident that Kelly was of a similar skill level as Eve. As they played, Eve tried to think of any information that she could elicit from Kelly that might unearth any useful information. There were only so many questions to ask the three people with alibis that couldn't possibly have been responsible for harming Art. She was having a hard time thinking of anything to ask as she found herself more and more engrossed in the interesting chess match.

Eventually, it was Kelly that asked a question. "Is your boyfriend finally making his move?"

Eve looked up. "Excuse me? My boyfriend?"

"Yeah. The sheriff. Isn't he your boyfriend?"

"No."

"Oh. I thought he was. He acts like it."

"No," Eve repeated. "Not my boyfriend. What did you mean by 'making his move'?"

"I was wondering if he was finally arresting Margo. I thought maybe that's why you didn't go into the office with her."

"We can only hope, right?" Eve replied with a sad little laugh. The she quietly asked, "Did you see Margo leave her room and walk outside during 4 and 5 yesterday?"

"No," said Kelly, matching the hushed volume. "I've thought and thought about it, but I didn't see her. It doesn't mean that she didn't walk through the room, but I don't remember seeing her. I've asked Sheila and Henry too, but we weren't paying much attention to who was coming and going during that time. I'm sure we would be better witnesses if we had been told in advance to pay attention. I wish at least one of us could remember seeing her so we could help."

"You think she did it?"

"It has to be her."

"Why is that?"

"Because it would take a cruel person to use an innocent horse as a weapon. I just can't imagine a veterinarian— a person who has dedicated their life to the care of animals— to use one in such a heartless manner. I just can't imagine it. Or, at least, I don't want to. A vet just can't be the one who did this and Margo's the only one that's not a vet."

Eve and Kelly contemplated that thought in silence as they continued with their chess game. Eve was surprised at how lost she was becoming in the match. As it became more complicated, each move was taking longer to be decided and executed. A significant amount of time had passed before Eve reminded herself she had been trying to think of things to ask Kelly. She forced herself back into conversation, picking up where they left off, even though it had been a long time. "Lorenzo's not a vet," she said.

"Huh?" Kelly said with confusion as she looked up from the chess board after making a move.

"You said Margo was the only one here that isn't a veterinarian, but Lorenzo isn't either."

"But he's a horse trainer. He loves horses as much as we do."

"You think so? I heard that you said it is common knowledge that Lorenzo will do anything for money. You don't think that could extend to something like throwing a tumbleweed into a stable with an unsuspecting veterinarian and a troubled horse?"

"Oh no!" Kelly gasped. "I meant he'll do married socialites, not murder!"

"Okay, I just wanted clarification," Eve said as she began moving her bishop with trepidation and then reconsidered.

"I don't know him well or anything," said Kelly, "but I'm under the impression that he's a lover not a killer. I feel so bad if I started a ghastly rumor. Oh no!" she exclaimed causing Eve to look up at her. Kelly looked horrified. "He's not going to get arrested or go to jail for something I said, is he? I was just gossiping!"

"Don't worry," Eve said dismissively as she looked back down at the chess board. "He's not going to be arrested."

"Are you sure?"

"I'm sure."

"But… but…" Kelly stammered.

Eve was still looking down at the chess pieces as she reassuringly said to Kelly, "Don't worry. I promise, Lorenzo's not getting arrested."

"But…" Kelly said again as she raised her arm and pointed across the room.

Eve followed her finger to see Sheriff Strider leading Lorenzo into the office. Eve was dismayed that she somehow missed Margo leaving the office and Sheriff Strider collecting Lorenzo. She had been paying far too much attention to the chess game. Perhaps, like Kelly, if she had been told in advance to pay attention…

Lorenzo walked into the office while Sheriff Strider hung back. He was looking across the room giving Eve a look that telegraphed, 'Are you coming?'

Eve muttered an apology to Kelly and practically ran across the room.

## Chapter Twenty-Three

The interest that had caused Eve to almost run across the room dissipated quickly when she heard the questions Sheriff Strider had for Lorenzo. They were routine questions about his unaccounted whereabouts during the time that Art was killed. Lorenzo said he was in his room some of the time and then in the dining room and then outside to get something from his car. It was the same information that he had given to Deputy Navarro yesterday evening. Eventually, Eve's interest disappeared completely and she started thinking about her chess conversation with Colin. She was abruptly forced to pay attention to the interview when the sheriff surprised her by asking, "Do you have any further questions, Ms. Cordova?"

"Me?" she asked. "Yes, actually. I do." She looked intently at Lorenzo as she asked, "Did you let Colin into the CARED fundraiser in Kentucky?"

Lorenzo matched the intensity of her gaze for a moment before letting out a laugh. "Yes," he answered with an easy smile. "Did he tell you?"

"No," replied Eve. "He said that he paid someone to

let him in. I thought it must be someone that he had previously known, so it would probably be someone from Arizona. I considered that it might be Burt. But my guess is that if Burt and Colin knew each other previously and Burt was willing to do it, he would have done it for free. But Colin said he paid someone to let him in. And you are the guy who people pay to do things, right?"

"Everyone needs to make a living," Lorenzo said with such a staggeringly sexy stare that Eve found herself weakened by it and suddenly speechless.

Luckily, Sheriff Strider was immune to Lorenzo's superpower. "There's a line between making a living and criminal activity," he said harshly.

Lorenzo's charming smile vanished quickly. "Listen," he began earnestly. "I am from a big family, a big poor family. I am not embarrassed to do what I need to do to keep shirts on their backs, food in their bellies, and occasionally give them the extravagance of being able to go to the doctor every once in a while. This isn't the life I envisioned for myself but it's the one I have, and I take advantage of it. When someone offers me money to do something, I can't turn it down. I have to think of my family."

Now that Lorenzo had ditched the sexy smile, Eve could speak again. "It's not to get fancy, expensive boots?"

"They were a gift. It's rude to not accept a gift."

"And for what you do you need to look good," Eve suggested.

Lorenzo's smile came back as he said, "It doesn't hurt."

The sheriff cleared his throat before saying, "So, Mr. Dominguez, you admit that you are the guy that people come to when they want something done."

"Yes. But I don't do anything illegal. Questionable maybe, but not illegal." Lorenzo's smile broadened as he said, "Well, not very illegal."

"Like getting paid to sneak someone into a fundraiser."

"Yes. And to be completely honest, the fundraiser was my idea. Colin came to me and asked me if I could connect him with some of my wealthy clients. I said no. I've spent a lot of time cultivating my relationships and I wasn't about to let Colin come in asking them for money. But I thought he might do it behind my back anyway, using my name and tarnishing my reputation. Colin… well, let's just say, he lacks finesse. I really didn't want him talking to my clients. Honestly, I didn't trust him. I had this fundraiser in Kentucky that I was going to, so I suggested he go out there and try getting his funding from people outside of my network. And yes, I made him pay me for the service to let him into the fundraiser. I wasn't helping him out of the goodness of my heart. I was trying to get him out of my way."

"Okay," said Eve. "That's the only question I had. Thanks."

Lorenzo started to rise from his chair.

"Wait, Mr. Dominguez," said Sheriff Strider.

Lorenzo returned to his seated position.

"I have another question," said the sheriff. "The question that I thought Ms. Cordova was going to ask you. Since you are the man who people pay to do things… Did you recently use the woodchipper to shred papers for Mrs. Wells? She wouldn't tell me who she got to do that for her."

"Oh!" said Eve. "Sorry. I didn't ask him that because I already know it was him."

"You do?" said Lorenzo and the sheriff in unison with the same shocked expression.

"Yes," replied Eve. "In fact, it's the reason I'm 99% sure you aren't the person who killed Art."

The expressions of the two men in the room changed from the same shocked expression to two very different expressions. Lorenzo's face relaxed with contentment, while the sheriff's face contorted with confusion.

"I smelled your cologne in the woodchipper pen," Eve explained to Lorenzo. "I realized that if your cologne was strong enough to linger in an open-air environment, I certainly would have noticed its smell lingering in the stables if you had been the one in there with the tumbleweed. But I didn't smell it so it must not have been you."

"Good!" Lorenzo said with a big smile as he leaned back and clasped his hands behind his head. "So… since I'm not a suspect anymore, do you want my help?"

"Your help?" asked the sheriff.

"Sure. Why not?"

"Are you under the impression that I'm going to pay you as some sort of consulting detective?"

"That's not necessary. I'm already getting paid."

"What?" Eve blurted. "Paid? By whom?"

"By Dr. Hudson."

"Olive is paying you?" Eve asked in disbelief. "To do what?"

"To spy on everyone."

Lorenzo's reveal was met with silence. Eve's silence was born from surprise, but she could tell the sheriff's silence was a product of anger. He was furious, she could tell, but only because she knew him so well. He was skilled at quietly processing his anger. Eve thought that it was a very attractive quality. She was not a fan of adult temper tantrums.

Finally, Eve said, "Why?"

"Why what?"

"Why did she ask you to spy on everyone?"

"To help her find out who killed Art, of course. She overheard me talking to Kelly and was impressed with my superior powers of persuasion. She thought I would be an asset. She wanted another pair of eyes and ears and thought I might be able to unearth hidden information." Oblivious to the sheriff's extreme disapproval, Lorenzo turned to him and casually asked, "So, what do you want to know? I'm a very good judge of character. I can give you my opinions on these people if you'd like."

Eve wondered if she should step in and explain that Sheriff Strider was not interested in the conclusions of Lorenzo's civilian snooping. But before she made a decision on how best to politely decline his offer, the sheriff surprised her by saying, "Tell me whatever you have found to be of interest." He glanced over at Eve for a half second before adding, "If you think that would be okay with Dr. Hudson, of course."

Eve almost laughed out loud.

"I'm sure she wouldn't mind," said Lorenzo. "She's sharing all her intel with you anyway, isn't she? After all, we're all on the same team, trying to find out who did this horrid thing to Art, right? I mean, I might as well tell you directly."

"Sounds good," said the sheriff. "Since you are such a good judge of character, who do you think did it?"

"If I was a betting man, I'd put my money on the wife."

"Yes, she seems to be the frontrunner in this race," said the sheriff. "Do you have a second-place choice?"

"No. The rest are neck and neck right now."

"What do you think of their characters?"

"I don't see Colin as a killer, but I could see him making a miscalculation that would cause a murder. Jessica could be a killer. She's got fire in her. Reid's a phony and—"

"Tell me more about that, about Reid being a phony."

Eve's look of disapproval went unnoticed since the sheriff avoided looking at her. She couldn't believe him. After all, Lorenzo had just said he thought Jessica could be a killer, but Sheriff Strider ignored that to focus on the subject of Reid.

"I talked to him as much as I could during the trivia game since we were on the same team. I got the impression that he talks a bigger game than he can deliver. I was asking him questions about his job and his answers didn't satisfy me. I think he's overrated. I understand the horses I train. I get to know them, their personalities, their interests, their dislikes, their relationships with other horses and with certain people. After talking to him, I am certain that I have a better understanding of a horse's psyche than he does. But he's rich and famous for being able to communicate with horses on a higher level than other people? Not me. He's not better than me. I'm sure of it."

"That sounds like professional jealousy to me," Eve couldn't help but pointing out.

"I suppose it is," Lorenzo admitted. "It should be me. I should be the one making Aspen chalet money. Anyway, who else does that leave? Oh yes, Burt. Burt, who was friends with Art. He's one to watch."

"Have you witnessed any strange behavior from him?" asked the sheriff.

"No," said Lorenzo. "But he plays it pretty cool. I think you'd need something special to trip him up."

"And what about Dr. Hudson?"

Lorenzo raised an eyebrow. "Olive? She didn't do it. She's trying to find out who did. We both are. But, like I said, my money would be on Margo."

"Any particular reason?" asked the sheriff.

"Lots of them."

"Such as?"

"She not only asked me to shred documents out at the woodchipper."

"What?" Eve asked with horror. "What else did she want you to use the woodchipper for?"

Lorenzo chuckled, "No, no, my friend. Nothing like that. She knew that the woodchipper pen was where you put the tumbleweeds. She wanted me to bring a piece of tumbleweed back to the hotel and put it in Colin's room."

"To frame him for murder?" Eve asked with a

different kind of horror. "And you agreed to that?"

"No," Lorenzo replied calmly. "I said she asked me. I did not agree to it. I told her I would shred the papers and that was all. Of course, Olive paid me first, so she got to read the presentations before I shredded them. But I did keep my word to Margo, I destroyed the papers." He laughed. "See, I'm even honest when I'm acting as a double agent! I did what Margo paid me to do. But framing someone for murder is not something I would ever do."

The sheriff stared at Lorenzo judgmentally for a moment before saying, "You said that you had multiple reasons for suspecting Mrs. Wells. Why else?"

"I think she's faking her ankle injury," replied Lorenzo.

"Why would she do that?"

"I don't know. To play us? To get sympathy?" Lorenzo suggested. "Maybe she's smart enough to realize she can't get any sympathy with her personality," he added with a little humor.

Very seriously, Eve suggested, "Maybe she's smart enough to get away with murder."

## Chapter Twenty-Four

After Lorenzo left the office, Sheriff Strider released his pent-up frustration with a loud growling exhale. He followed it by saying, "I need to have a talk with Dr. Hudson."

"Olive?" Eve asked incredulously. "Not Margo? Lorenzo just told us she was actively trying to frame someone for this murder! I'm guessing that's not something Margo divulged to you during her interview."

"I know, but that didn't surprise me, finding out about Dr. Hudson's actions did. I want to speak with her immediately." He looked into Eve's eyes and pointedly added, "Alone."

"Hey! Don't blame me," Eve said defensively. "I specifically told her to not step on your toes."

"Well, my toes are stepped on. You don't hire a suspect to help you investigate! And to me, SHE is a suspect. So, a suspect hires another suspect to investigate or just muddy the waters? Or is she…"

"Or is she what?"

Sheriff Strider put his hands to his temples. "I don't know," he said with exasperation. "I honestly don't know what she's thinking. And I'm not blaming you. But I still want to speak with her alone."

Eve nodded with understanding. She liked Olive. She would definitely give the meeting a friendly atmosphere. "I knew that 'I'm too adorable to be taken seriously' line would come back to haunt me." Eve stood. "I'll go get her."

Eve was not surprised to find Olive in the lobby with Reid, Sheila, Kelly, Henry, and Colin, but the general mood did surprise her. This group of usually friendly people seemed uncharacteristically depressed. The forced togetherness was further souring the already stressed ambience.

Eve told Olive that the sheriff wanted to see her in the office. Olive got up out of her chair and left just as Reid walked over to the piano and sat down. As he started playing, Eve abandoned her plan to seek refuge in her suite. Reid's beautiful music instantly soothed her. Eve slid down into Olive's chair and listened to the intoxicating sounds. After a few minutes, she realized that it was not only she that was enjoying the music. It seemed to cast a pleasurable spell over everyone in the hotel. The people in the lobby; Sheila, Kelly, Henry, and Colin, seemed to visibly relax as the music enveloped them. Jessica came out of her room upstairs, leaned against the balcony railing, and watched Reid play below. Any signs of her lingering distrust and anger seemed to have vanished as she watched Reid play.

Eve was not only thrilled to finally hear the piano's music filling the hotel, but she was truly mesmerized by Reid's talent. She didn't know how long she had been staring at his quick, agile fingers dancing upon the piano keys when she felt a hand on her shoulder. She looked up to find Sheriff Strider looking down at her. She realized that she must have been sitting there for quite some time if he was done with Olive's interview. She wondered how long the sheriff had been watching her watch Reid play the piano.

"Can I talk to you?" asked Sheriff Strider.

Even though he was right next to her, she could barely hear him over the music. She nodded and followed him into the office.

Sheriff Strider shut the door and immediately said, "You know you can trust me, right?"

"Yes, of course."

"I mean it."

"I know," Eve said, although she didn't really know anything at the moment. She certainly didn't know what was going on.

"I don't think you do."

"I do."

"You do?"

"I'm sorry. I'm lost. What's happening right now?"

"I'm tired of playing this game," he said.

"What game?"

"They one where we pretend that you're not lying to me."

"About what?" Eve asked, although the formation of the lump in her throat suggested she knew exactly what this was about.

"Why didn't you just tell me that you had Wes remove Blaze from the property?"

"I—"

"...don't trust me."

"I trust you! But... you... You are the law. I didn't want to put you in a position where you had to choose between the law and me."

"And you think that you are the opposite of the law? You are one of the strictest rule followers that I know. I remember you once complaining to me for fifteen minutes about the people who enter into the post office parking lot the wrong way."

"It's clearly marked EXIT ONLY. I still don't know why you don't arrest those people," she said with a hint of humor.

The sheriff remained serious as he said, "Because law enforcement is like any other aspect in life in that you have to choose your battles."

"I didn't tell you about Blaze because I didn't want to implicate you."

"I understand that, and I appreciate your attempt to give me plausible deniability, but I want you to trust me. I want you to trust me like I trust you. I have known you for quite a while now and I trust you. Completely."

"Completely?"

"Yes. Completely."

"Oh," Eve said. "I don't know if that's a good idea. I don't know if I even trust myself completely."

"I guess you don't have to. That's what I'm here for."

Eve wondered if she had stopped breathing or not. She wondered if she had forgotten how to breathe. She most certainly had forgotten how to speak. She was reeling from one of the most touching sentiments she had ever heard. *He trusts me completely? He trusts me more than I trust myself? Wow... Wow.* Eve forced herself to say something, so she said the only word she remembered, the only word bouncing around in her head. She said, "Wow."

The sheriff ignored her dazed response and continued with his speech. "I don't want you confusing me for my job. Yes, I believe in what I do so that I can hold the bad accountable, but I don't want you thinking that I'm an inflexible monster. I don't want you to think that I revel in punishing the innocent people, and animals, who get caught in the crossfire of wicked people."

Eve felt guilty for keeping the truth from him, for treating him like the enemy. But she had had her reasons. "But you have to follow the rules," she said as a pathetic attempt to justify her actions.

"I am comfortable bending the rules when I see fit. I trust you enough to tell you that and I want you to trust me enough to know that."

She looked into his eyes as she earnestly said, "Okay."

"So, the next time you want to do something stupid or questionable, just let me in on it. I'll have your back. I promise."

"Okay," she repeated. Eve waited until she was sure that she remembered how to breathe before asking, "Are you going to tell me what Olive said?"

"Yes, but please, remember that she's a suspect and could be lying about anything or everything."

"I know, I know, but I like her. I trust her. Not completely," she added shyly. "I think I trust her. So, what did she say?"

"She said that she thought it would be okay to hire Mr. Dominguez as an informant because she believed him to be innocent. She also noticed that his cologne smell was not lingering in the stables when Art was found."

"Brilliant minds…," said Eve. "Except, she's more brilliant because she figured that out long before I did. She even asked me if I had smelled anything that wasn't supposed to be there. I thought it was the strangest question at the time. I guess she didn't explain herself because she decided to secretly hire Lorenzo to help her. What a scamp."

"A scamp? Or a very intelligent woman who has been playing us this whole time?" suggested the sheriff.

"Hopefully, a scamp. Did she say anything else?"

"She also told me what Mr. Dominguez had discovered during his investigations. But it was all gossipy stuff of no interest to me."

"Did he really tell Olive when Margo asked him to destroy the papers?"

"Yes. She verified his story. He told her about the request, and she asked to see the papers before he destroyed them."

"So, she read about his drug reveal. Did she say if she had known about it already?"

"She said no, she did not know any specifics about it before reading the presentation, but she said it didn't surprise her. She explained the technical aspects of the presentation that we didn't grasp. Basically, the chemical compound appears to act as a type of steroid without the usual ill effects. She said that makes sense because he was always looking for ways to help horses with muscular atrophy problems. In the past these animals would be put down, but Dr. Wells's wanted to find a way to save, extend, and improve their lives."

"Okay," Eve said, not trying to hide the disappointment in her voice. "That's nice but is it a murder motive?"

"I don't know. Anything can be a motive for murder. What might appear like nothing to us could be an earth-shattering event for someone else. Despite your and Dr. Hudson's noses, I still like 'Mr. Suave' for this."

"You mean Lorenzo? You still think he did it?"

"Colin McCullough pays him to sneak him into a fundraiser. Margo Wells pays him to shred papers. Olive Hudson pays him to spy on everyone. Are we sure that someone didn't pay him to commit murder?"

Eve noticed that he used the word 'we' as if they were making decisions together, as if her opinion was just as important as his, as sheriff. "Pretty sure. Almost positive. But even if he did, you'd have to find out who hired him."

"Oh," said the sheriff, "I also found out another piece of interesting information from Dr. Hudson. But now that I think about it, if it was information that Lorenzo fed her and he's in on it…"

"What is it?" she asked hopefully.

"Margo is the one who contacted Dr. Spurlock to attempt to reach out to Dr. Wells to invest in the new drug. She obviously thought her husband's new drug invention was worth a lot of money, and when money is involved, motives abound."

"I've been wondering this whole time why Margo was

even here. I guess it was to broker a deal between Art and Gabriel, to set herself up financially. That makes sense."

"Let's see if Dr. Spurlock will corroborate his 'little birdie's' identity. Plus, one of my deputies also unearthed some new information that I'd like to ask Dr. Spurlock about."

"You're going to talk to him and not Margo?"

"Yes."

She asked, "Why not Margo?" and then regretted it. He had just been so nice to her and here she was second guessing him. She reminded herself that he was in charge, not her. "Never mind. Sorry. I'll go find Gabriel and bring him back."

"Thanks," said the sheriff with an intense look that Eve decided must be the physical embodiment of complete trust. It made her feel a little uneasy. She honestly couldn't tell if it was a good uneasy or a bad uneasy.

As she walked through the music-filled lobby looking for Gabriel, she wondered how she felt about being trusted completely. It was a lot of responsibility. She shook off the thought when she found Gabriel tucked in the corner of the dining room sifting through a pile of papers on the table in front of him.

"Ow," he muttered and looked at the blood on his finger before he stuck it into his mouth.

Eve cringed at the unsanitary act. "Are you okay?" she asked as she walked up to him.

Gabriel looked annoyed to be interrupted but said, "Yes, just a stupid papercut. The biggest argument for going paperless. They keep going on and on about the environment but what they should do is spearhead an anti-papercut campaign."

"What are you looking at? Horse racing bets?"

"I don't bet on horse racing," Gabriel scoffed.

"You said you bet on Reid's horses."

"That's not betting, that's an investment."

"Because his horses always win?"

"Yes. It's not betting if it's a sure thing."

"You must really believe in his psychological techniques."

"Of course not," said Gabriel. "You can't talk a horse into winning a race. That's ridiculous."

"But—"

"Did you want something?" Gabriel interrupted, not bothering to hide his impatience.

"The sheriff wants to see you."

Gabriel sighed loudly and gathered up his papers, putting them into his briefcase before following Eve to the office. He unceremoniously threw himself into the chair as he rudely said, "Now what?" to Sheriff Strider.

"I'm sorry, Dr. Spurlock. Is Dr. Wells's murder inconveniencing you?"

"Yes, actually," Gabriel replied. "Is that really the question you wanted to ask me? Seems like a waste."

"I don't have a limited number of questions," said Sheriff Strider. "You are not a genie granting me three wishes. In fact, you're not even granting me a reasonable amount of respect. I will ask you as many questions as I want. Understand?"

"Yes, fine. I'm finding this all rather tiresome. Let's get it over with. I'll tell you anything you want if it means that I can get on with my life. Ask away."

"Mrs. Wells is the one who asked you to come here, correct?"

"Yes."

"She wanted you to invest in her husband's drug?"

"Yes. She told me her husband was clueless when it came to the prospect of capitalizing on his creation. She wanted someone successful to help realize the full potential of profit."

"Do you think she killed her husband to keep that profit for herself?"

"I don't know. I don't know her. Not really. She had

just reached out to me about this investment opportunity. I was intrigued so I came. But I don't know her well enough to make an accusation of murder. Although, that seems to be the general consensus around here."

"It is?" Eve asked with interest.

"Yes. The rumor is that she is guilty and that she is going to try and make a break for it."

"Who did you hear that from?"

"Oh, that lady Sheila. But I would take it with a grain of salt. She's a gossip and everyone is going a little stir crazy being cooped up in here."

"Oh, okay," said Eve deep in contemplation.

"Is that all?" Gabriel asked.

"No," replied the sheriff. "I have another question about the Worthington horse racing collective."

"That again?"

"I just found out that they're under investigation."

"So?"

"They're under investigation for inhumane practices."

"So?"

"You are an investor in that collective."

"I invest in a lot of things."

"They were reported by an anonymous whistleblower."

"What does this have to do with the death of Art Wells?"

"Dr. Wells worked for them years ago."

"So?" Gabriel once again asked. "Lots of people have worked for them. I too worked for them many years ago for a short time."

"Did you work with Dr. Wells?"

"No. I told you that I had never met the man before this conference."

"Why did you leave the collective?"

"I got a better paying job."

"Well, Dr. Wells quit because he didn't like the practices of the operation. In recent years, he has dedicated his free time to helping animals in need."

"And?"

"Do you think Dr. Arthur Wells was the whistleblower?"

"How would I know?"

"Someone may have told you. In fact, they may have told you to come to this conference and take care of the problem."

"Oh," Gabriel chuckled darkly.

"Oh?"

"I see."

"You do?"

"Yes. You're delusional. You're trying to paint me as some sort of veterinarian investor by day and contract killer by night. Do you know how ridiculous that sounds?"

"Just because something sounds like a preposterous theory, it doesn't mean that it's not true."

"Maybe occasionally. But most of the time, if something sounds unbelievable, it is. If you want to find the murderer of Art Wells, I suggest you limit your pool of suspects to the people who actually knew the man."

## Chapter Twenty-Five

After Gabriel's interview, Eve and the sheriff both came to the sad conclusion that that they were absolutely nowhere in determining who killed Art or why. The sheriff got a phone call, and Eve was happy to take the opportunity to go do something productive. Esperanza didn't need her in the kitchen but suggested that Loretta might need help with the laundry. Eve liked that idea. Folding sheets sounded like a perfectly mindless yet useful activity to occupy herself with. The cold, short walk in the snow to the laundry room made her realize how claustrophobic she had been feeling cooped up in the hotel with everyone. It felt freeing to go to a separate building if only a few feet away. Eve found Loretta but unfortunately she didn't have anything for her to do either. Loretta was finishing up a load of Wes's laundry and only had a few socks to couple up before finishing her task.

"Ow," Loretta said as she looked at the small bubble of blood on her finger.

"I know laundry can be tedious," said Eve, "but I've never known it to be dangerous."

"It's a thorn," said Loretta as she used her non-bloodied fingers to wrestle it out of the sock. "Looks like a stupid tumbleweed thorn."

"Do the evils of tumbleweed never cease?" Eve said with exasperation. "I'll get you a bandage," she added quickly, thankful Loretta hadn't stuck her finger in her mouth. "I'll be right back."

On her way into the hotel to get some disinfectant and a bandage, Eve's mind started racing. She started to postulate theories. To her surprise, this time things started clicking into place. But she kept second guessing herself. Could the word "ow" really be what unraveled this mystery? *Ow*? It seemed too ridiculous, but it made sense. Everything was finally making sense. As she found the likely answers to her questions, Eve realized that Jessica had lied to her. Yes, she was sure that what Jessica told her was not true.

When Eve returned to the laundry room, she hurriedly applied the disinfectant and bandage to Loretta's finger and said, "Will you do me a favor? Well, will you do me a couple of favors? First, will you get the sheriff for me?"

Loretta came back with the sheriff, but he was engrossed in a phone call as they walked into the laundry room. When he ended the phone call, the sheriff and Eve locked eyes. In unison, they both said, "I think I know who did it."

After a short discussion, Eve was disappointed to learn that they were not talking about the same person. Then, after a long discussion, one in which discussing crossed the line into arguing more than once, Eve and the sheriff came up with a plan to see who was right.

After preparations had been made, Eve anxiously stood in the middle of the lobby as she watched Loretta up on the balcony go from room to room, knocking on each door and asking everyone to gather downstairs.

The guests assembled in the lobby with a communal

concerned seriousness. The air was thick with tension which made Roxie's arrival prancing in with an ice cream cone almost surreal. "What's going on?" she asked jovially and innocently, as if perhaps a sock hop was in the works. No one answered her.

"Is this everyone?" the sheriff asked Loretta.

"Everyone except for Olive and her," Loretta said as she pointed to the closed door of Margo's downstairs Suite C. "They didn't answer."

"Will you try Dr. Hudson's door again?" he asked Loretta.

Loretta headed back upstairs and the sheriff went to Suite C. He knocked loudly. "Margo Wells, open the door," he said even louder than the knock.

He had said it so loudly, in fact, that a few of the people in the lobby jumped with fright, including Roxie. Roxie's hand jerked which caused her ice cream cone to come into contact with Reid's cashmere cardigan sweater.

"I— I'm so sorry," Roxie said with a look of fright as she took turns looking at Reid's face and the pink ice cream clinging to the sweater.

"Roxie!" Eve said with agitation as she looked back to the sheriff and at Margo's closed door. "Why don't you offer to clean that for him?" she added distractedly with a wave of her hand.

"Oh, yeah," said Roxie. "Yeah, sorry. I'll clean it for you," she said to Reid. I'm so sorry."

Reid took off the cardigan and gave it to Roxie. Without another word, Roxie grabbed it and headed to the laundry room.

Eve inched her way over to Reid and said quietly, "I'm so sorry about that. Roxie's high spirts are delightful most of the time, but sometimes there's collateral damage."

The sheriff knocked again loudly on Margo's door. Everyone quieted, watched, and waited. He again called out to Margo to open the door but again, there was no answer. "I need the key to this room," Sheriff Strider barked at Eve.

It was Eve's turn to jump. She shot a perturbed look at no one in particular and walked to the front desk. She retrieved the key and opened Margo's door for the sheriff. She tried to follow him into the room but stopped when he turned and loudly said, "Stay back."

Eve balled her fists in a show of frustration but stayed where she was instructed. After a minute, the sheriff returned to the lobby.

"She's not here," the sheriff said with agitation.

"What?" Eve asked loudly. "Where is she?" she asked not bothering to keep the accusatory tone at bay.

"It looks like she went out the side door and drove away," he replied.

"Seriously?" Eve almost yelled. "She was here this whole time, and you didn't arrest her? And now she's gone? You let her get away! You should have arrested her hours ago!"

"I'm going after her," Sheriff Strider announced loudly before he stormed off.

He chose to cut through Suite C and leave the same way that Margo made her exit. Eve followed him to the door and looked to see for herself the evidence of Margo's footprints out to the snow and the snow-free parking space that had previously held Margo's SUV rental. Eve watched the sheriff clear the snow from his vehicle and slowly drive away in the ruts made by Margo. Eve angrily marched back into the lobby.

"Margo's really gone?" Gabriel asked immediately.

Eve looked at Gabriel long and hard before saying, "Yes. There are footprints out to the parking lot and tire tracks leading off the property. She had that big fancy SUV rental, so she made it out. I don't know how far she thinks she's going to make it but she's trying." Eve looked at Gabriel suspiciously, "Did you know she was going to try to leave?"

"Me?" Gabriel said with a step backward. "No. I

mean, I heard a rumor. But no. I didn't know. But I'm not surprised. It was only a matter of time before she was arrested. It was a smart move on her part."

"And the sheriff is going after her?" asked Colin.

Eve looked at Colin. "He's going to try," she said. "I can't believe we were too late. I'm so mad at him. I told him it was her. Time and time again I told him he should arrest her. He was so stubborn and waited too long. I'm so mad!"

"Don't worry, Eve," said Lorenzo. "I'm sure he'll catch up with her. But if she can make it through the snow, do you think we can too? I'd love to get out of here."

"No one's going anywhere," Reid said. "It's not safe."

"Yes," Eve projected to the room. "Everyone, just relax. We're all staying here for another night." Eve wished she could relax. But that wasn't possible. Her heart was thumping in her chest. She sighed as she watched Henry, Sheila, and Kelly retire to the couches; Lorenzo, Colin, Naiya, and Burt walk into the dining room; and Gabriel and Jessica walk upstairs to their rooms. Quietly to Reid, she said, "I do understand the desire to get out of here. I'm feeling a little rage induced claustrophobia myself. I'm so mad. The sheriff gave me this big speech about trusting me and then he didn't! Why didn't he just trust me?"

"Because he's a fool," Reid said kindly.

"I have to get out of here before I scream," Eve said helplessly.

"There's nowhere to go," said Reid logically. "Unless you'd like to slip into your apartment. I wouldn't mind a tour."

"No. I need space. I want to get out of this building and away from all these people. If Margo made it out to the road, I can make it across the property to the wine tasting room. In fact, I know I can, because I just had Loretta take our side-by-side ATV and bring over a few cases of wine from there."

"Well, now that's an idea. Would you like some company?"

"Sure. That sounds nice. Plus, if I get stuck in the snow, I should have someone with me."

"Unfortunately, that was the only sweater I brought," Reid said.

"Don't worry. I've got you covered."

As Eve and Reid descended the basement stairs to pick up a couple of parkas for their excursion to the wine tasting room, Eve wondered once again if Margo's fall down the stairs had been theatre and her limp, fake. Had she faked it just to get the downstairs suite with the exit door to make a getaway? Probably, she concluded. Eve mentally kicked herself for not thinking of that possibility earlier.

## Chapter Twenty-Six

The side-by-side was parked at the kitchen door where Loretta had left it. It was darker outside than Eve expected. The last remnants of hazy sunlight had completely disappeared. On the drive out to the winery with Reid, Eve made sure to keep the side-by-side's aggressive tires in the existing tracks and drive slowly. She made a point to not look too long at the tire tracks in the snow disappearing into the darkness towards Route 66. When they arrived at the dark winery, Eve switched the lights on, but Reid complained it was too bright. She agreed. As she lit some candles and set them on her favorite table, she said, "Thanks for coming out here with me. I needed to get out of there and get out of my head. Gabriel said that everyone was going stir crazy. I didn't realize that I would be joining the ranks. Plus, I hate to admit it, but I'm worried about the sheriff."

"Oh? I thought you were mad at him," Reid said.

"I am. We had disagreements on how best to deal with Margo. And I'm still annoyed because if our discussion hadn't taken so long, Margo wouldn't have got away. He should have listened to me! I am mad. But that doesn't mean I'm not worried about him. The roads are icy and dangerous. But let's change the subject. Sit, relax." Reid sat as Eve turned the overhead lights off. She then took one of the candles to make her way over to the bar. "After all, I wanted to tell you," she said to him from across the room, "the eagle has landed." She walked behind the bar, opened a bottle of Pinot Noir, and returned to the table with two glasses and an inviting smile.

"Blaze, you mean?" asked Reid.

"Yes." Eve poured them each a glass. She held her glass up and said, "To a successful mission."

"Here, here," he said as he clinked her glass. He took a large sip of wine.

"Thank you for your help with Blaze," Eve said. "Wes drove straight through. I don't know how he did it. But he finally got there. He said the property that you arranged for Blaze to live at is beautiful and the owners are lovely. Well, maybe he didn't use the word 'lovely,' that's not one of his regular words. Or maybe he did, he's deliriously tired. The point is, he's happy with the people and the place. And most importantly, it's tumbleweed free. They're putting Wes up in their guest house until he catches up on his sleep. Thank you so much."

"I was happy to help find a new home for Blaze. It is a sign that everything is working out the way that it should."

Eve took a sip of wine and was surprised at how comfortable she felt all of a sudden. Getting the bottle of wine from behind the bar had calmed her and the sip of wine calmed her further. She smiled at Reid and said, "I was so nervous arranging my first fugitive transport. I just sent Wes out with Blaze but didn't know where they we're going to go. It was horrible. And then it started to snow! I was so glad that Wes and Blaze got out when they did. I was so stressed. But then you came along and saved the day. You were a godsend, so helpful, so chivalrous."

This awarded her a toothy, proud smile. "Anytime,"

he said. He raised his glass again in celebration and took another sip.

She tried to smile back but couldn't. "Sorry," she said with a shake of her head. "I'm preoccupied. I just can't believe Margo got away. I'm so mad at myself that I didn't insist the sheriff arrest her earlier. I knew she was up to something."

"I think everyone assumed it was her," Reid said.

"But I knew she was hiding something! I just couldn't prove it."

"Don't beat yourself up, it's not your fault," said Reid kindly.

"There were things that just didn't make sense to me," Eve continued, "like how Margo had such expensive things when everyone, including she, agreed that Art and Margo had no money. I determined she must be doing something despicable to get extra cash."

"What do you think she was doing?"

*Here we go*, Eve thought as she took a deep breath. "Blackmail."

"Oh." Reid slowly sipped his wine.

"And do you know who I think she was blackmailing?"

"No. Who?"

Eve set down her wine glass and took another deep breath. "You."

Reid stiffened. "Pardon me?"

"You can be honest with me, Reid. Come on," she said with an easy laugh, surprising herself. "You didn't help me relocate Blaze out of the goodness of your heart. You were getting rid of the murder weapon. You killed Art."

"Eve! Being blackmailed? Committing murder? How could you possibly think these things of me?"

"Because it's true."

"Art was my friend! You know that Margo did it. That's why she ran away. Why are you accusing me? This is preposterous and quite honestly hurtful."

"Relax, Reid. I'm fine with the 'Margo did it' story. You were being honest when you told me that she could have killed her husband. She could have. She didn't, but she could have."

"I…" Reid began but faltered.

"She's a bad person," Eve said. "She deserves to have this pinned on her. Don't you agree?"

"Yes, I do. Because she did it."

Eve shook her head. "Jessica told me that what happened to her horse 17 years ago had nothing to do with what happened to my horse yesterday, but she was wrong. The use of Blaze's fear to kill Art has everything to do with Fearless's death." When Reid stayed quiet, Eve continued. "I made Jessica tell me what happened. She told me that Art confessed to using his new experimental drug on Fearless all those years ago. Art was reticent but you encouraged him and when he wouldn't do it, you took the needle and did it yourself."

"I believed in the genius of my friend and colleague. Being supportive isn't a crime."

"Using experimental drugs is."

"Yes, I realize that. But we were trying to help a sick horse. I already told you that Art was not responsible for Fearless's death. Fearless was just too far gone. It was his time."

"Yes, you said that you knew for a fact that Art was not responsible for Jessica's horse dying. Was it because you have used that exact same drug on other horses with great success?"

Reid smiled. "Yes. I admit it. I've used it many times. It's perfectly safe, and surprisingly easy to manufacture. It's a miracle drug."

"But after the death of Fearless, Art became so cautious that it took him almost another 20 years of experiments to feel comfortable revealing his miracle drug."

"Yes."

"And you couldn't have him reveal the drug, right? That would have blown up your scam. You had an undetectable steroid alternative to dope racehorses. All you had to do was secretly give your horse patients the drug and weave your web of lies about being some sort of genius who understands the psyche of horses. That was your life, your reputation, your future. You couldn't let Art take that away from you. Even if people didn't make the connection between you and Art and started suspecting you of stealing the formula from him years ago, your career would be over. You would have no magic drug. The horse racing industry would start testing racehorses for the new drug. Your days of pretending to be an unparalleled horse psychiatrist would be over. Your money, your fame, all gone."

"That's a very interesting story," said Reid.

"It's not a story. It's true, unlike your entire career. You know, just a little while ago Gabriel said that talking a horse into winning a race was a ridiculous concept. I kept thinking about that. It is ridiculous and yet you gaslighted the entire horse racing world into believing it. And you killed to keep your secret."

"You have no proof," he said casually with a smug smile.

"That's where you're wrong. I do have proof. Margo was right when she told you that you shouldn't wipe your nose on your sleeve. That's how I know you did it."

"Excuse me?"

"I have the smoking gun, or rather the thorned cashmere cardigan."

"What?" he asked with a flash of fear in his eyes.

"I had Loretta tell Roxie to run into you with her ice cream cone so that she could take your cardigan on the pretense of cleaning it. Your sweater is the evidence. When you wiped your nose on your sleeve and you said 'ow' you blamed it on your nose getting raw, but it's not raw, not at all. It would be noticeable on that fair skin of yours. The pain you felt was from a thorn stuck in your sweater from when you picked up the tumbleweed to cause Art's death. The thorn is still embedded in the sleeve."

"So? I have a thorn in my sleeve. Perhaps…," he paused awkwardly, betraying his crumbling confidence. "Perhaps I picked up a tumbleweed to help you clean up the property."

"Everyone witnessed you unwilling to do that. Both you and Gabriel watched a tumbleweed roll right by you. The one you later used, by the way. No, that won't work to explain it away."

Reid silently shook his head.

"There's no point in denying it," Eve continued calmly. "I know that you have spent a lot of time planning your innocent remarks and constructing your statement, but a better solution is presenting itself to you. It's time to pivot."

His eyes sparkled in the candlelight as the corner of his mouth twitched upward. "What exactly are you proposing?"

"An alliance, of course."

"I like the sound of that."

"You are a businessman and I'm a businesswoman. I'm sure we can come to an arrangement."

"Blackmail? Is that all women know how to do? First Margo, and now you?"

"So, I was right. She was blackmailing you. She was eavesdropping on the conversation you and Art were having at the fundraiser last year. And although Art believed your lies about not using his drug formula for all these years, Margo did not. She suspected you were indeed using the formula you stole from Art to dope your racehorses. That's when she started blackmailing you, after the fundraiser. Olive mentioned that Margo was wearing an outdated gown to the fundraiser. She didn't have the expensive things that she has now. That must have been when the blackmail started."

"That's all she had on me? She was just guessing? She told me she had some proof that I had been using Art's drug on my horses. I had been paying her off for nothing?"

"Well, not nothing. She knew the truth."

"But without proof, it was an empty threat. Margo didn't know anything about the chemical properties of the drug. Who was she to make any claims about it? She would have come off as a jealous crazy lady. I wouldn't have worried about it. But that's not the blackmailing of which I was speaking."

"What do you mean?"

"Margo was blackmailing me anew."

"She was?"

"It doesn't matter. What is it that you want?"

Eve needed Reid to say more. She tried again. "What was she blackmailing you for now?"

"All that matters is that Margo is convicted of Art's murder. So, do you want to help me do that?"

"Well, since you are planning to have Margo arrested, you're not actually going to pay her. So, you can just give me the money that you never planned on giving her."

"And that's it?"

"You could also give me your undying affection," Eve said with a coy look and a flutter of feminine eye batting. It made her sick to her stomach, but she needed to get Reid comfortable with her, really comfortable.

"Maybe I will. You may be the perfect woman for me."

"So, the drug stays your secret, and Margo gets convicted of Art's murder. That's the plan right? I can help sell that story for you. Do we have a deal?"

"Hmmm. The sheriff does like you. Having you on my side would be an asset."

"Then to our alliance," she said as she held up her glass. After he politely clinked it, she said, "But before I talk to the sheriff on your behalf, I'll need to know everything that happened so that I can be prepared. I need the truth so that I can be properly prepared to pivot with my fiction if required. I need to have the right answers to the questions that will be asked."

He looked at her cautiously. At least a full minute passed before he finally replied. "What do you want to know?"

"Was Margo blackmailing you because she knew that you murdered Art?"

"Yes, she saw me walking to the stables with the tumbleweed. I made sure to scan the grounds to make sure no one was around watching me, but apparently I didn't think of looking up at the hotel balcony. Of course, she had that brown dress on and probably blended into the building. It was unfortunate that I was seen, but at least it was by the most morally bankrupt person here. The one person I knew I could manipulate with the promise of money."

"She knew and she didn't care? She just used it as leverage to get more money? She really is evil." Eve immediately regretted her goody goody outburst. She was supposed to be playing the part of seductress blackmailer. Luckily, it didn't seem to be a red flag to Reid.

"I know, she is. She wanted Colin convicted so that, not only could she get Art's life insurance money, but she also wanted me to get my money back from him so that I could give it to her."

"That's reprehensible."

"Yes. That's why I came up with a different plan, a better plan than trying to pin it on innocent Colin McCullough. That was too much of a leap anyway. He's a boy scout. I decided to pin it in on someone more fitting. Someone who everyone already suspected."

"Margo."

"I agreed to her blackmailing terms as long as she left as soon as possible. All she could see were dollar signs and a new life in a new country. She didn't realize that it would make her look guilty and would be as good as a confession to law enforcement. There was no way she could make it out of the country before they caught her. Especially since I told Sheila I heard Margo was the murderer and she was going to try and leave. As I suspected, Sheila started spreading that rumor like wildfire. Everyone thought Margo was guilty anyway. And Margo has always been a repugnant woman, she deserves it."

Eve held her breath, not wanting to disrupt Reid's confession. But when he paused she felt she needed to prod him. She needed him to say more, to be more specific. But just as she was about to say something Reid laughed loudly before continuing.

"You know," he said. "I didn't mean to kill Art. That is to say, it wasn't my plan, not my original plan. I just, you know, pivoted. I actually came here to get rid of Margo!" He laughed and took a sip of wine.

"Oh really?" Eve said with a smile that was becoming harder and harder to force.

"I had had enough of her. I refused to pay her blackmail anymore. When Art asked me to come to the conference, I thought it was a great opportunity to make some changes. After I got here, Margo told me about Art's plan to unveil his new drug. Which, of course, was the same as the old drug. My drug. You were right. I couldn't let Art blow up my life like that. I'd be ruined. I realized it was time to pivot. I didn't know exactly what I was going to do until Art told me that he was going to go see the problem horse and I remembered that tumbleweed Colin picked up. It was inspired. Of course, I still had the problem with Margo, but I figured she'd get a life insurance settlement and probably remarry some poor rich bastard. Her claims about me using a mystery drug that she couldn't explain wouldn't amount to anything. Without Art's knowledge, her claims would be unfounded. I would say she was hysterical after her husband's bizarre and tragic death, yadda yadda yadda. But unfortunately, Margo saw me heading to the stables with the tumbleweed. When she blackmailed me again I started thinking my original idea had merit."

Eve couldn't hide her look of disgust. To her surprise, Reid laughed again.

"Don't worry, I didn't kill her. I needed a patsy for Art's murder more than I needed that satisfaction. I paid her to destroy any evidence she had of the drug and then leave. Rather, I told her I would pay her if she left. I was never going to, of course. I certainly wasn't going to make another payment, not after I already paid Colin."

"Did Colin see you too? I thought it strange that you gave him such a hefty donation to his sanctuary."

"I'm embarrassed to say that was a quarter of a million-dollar mistake on my part. I had just come back from the stables, having engineered my rather clever removal of Art. As soon as I came back to the hotel, Colin approached me about donating to his sanctuary. I thought he was shaking me down. I assumed he had seen me walking to the stables with the tumbleweed. I panicked and shut him up as fast as I could. I did a wire transfer right then and there. It was my only mistake. But it's not a mistake that will get me caught. In fact, it just makes me look like a big-hearted philanthropist."

"So, Margo was the only one who saw you."

"Yes, but I think I turned things around pretty nicely. She makes the perfect scapegoat. All I had to do was talk her into faking that fall to get the downstairs suite with the external door out to the parking lot and then, when the time was right, play the piano to mask the sound of her driving away. No one will believe her when she tries to tell the cops that it was me, especially after her public insistence on it being Colin. Everyone will just think she's accusing everyone one by one to see if something sticks. It'll just make her appear more guilty. I must say, offering to pay her off and getting her to leave set her up quite nicely. She's a greedy idiot. She's on her way to Brazil but I'm sure she'll get picked up soon enough."

"She did get picked up," said Eve.

"She did? Where? How do you know?"

"The sheriff told me. Her SUV slid off the road about five miles outside of Sandmat. Deputy Navarro was the one who got the call and recognized her immediately. He has her detained at the jail in the sheriff's station."

Reid looked thoughtful as he nodded his head and said, "Hmmm. Good."

"Yes, very good," Eve said as she stood.

"Wait," said Reid. "When did the sheriff tell you that? We were all there when we found out Margo had left and then he left to go find her."

"Oh, that was just for show," said Eve as she walked over to the light switch by the door. "By then we already knew she had been picked up."

"For show? For whose benefit?"

"For yours." Eve paused and turned around to face Reid in the candlelight. "The sheriff got the call that Margo had left and was picked up at the same time that I started to wonder about a thorn in your sleeve. He was sure Margo was the murderer; I was sure it was you. In a way, I guess we were both right. And you know what? I'm sure that Margo will make an excellent witness against you after she listens to the recording. She'll be more than happy to cut a deal and testify at the trial of her almost murderer. But then again, with the recording, nobody needs to give Margo any sort of deal. She can be charged with accessory after the fact or whatever it's called. Hmmm. Things really are working out the way they're supposed to."

"Recording?" Reid asked unsurely.

Eve turned back to the wall and flipped all the light switches on, making the room suddenly and glaringly bright. "You can come out now," she called to the only reason she had felt comfortable having a candlelit drink with a murderer.

Sheriff Strider rose from his position crouched behind the bar and trained a gun at Reid. Sheriff Strider started a slow walk towards them as he said, "You were right about one thing, Dr. Tolliver. The sheriff does like her. That's why he went along with this crazy plan of hers."

Reid jumped up into a standing position and took a step closer to the door that Eve was blocking. "There's no recording," Reid said frantically.

"Yes, there is," said Olive as she emerged from the adjoining barrel room with Ramon.

"I put a wireless microphone in the flowers on the table," said Ramon. "Thank you for speaking so directly and clearly. The quality is great and has already been uploaded to the cloud."

"Yes, it was a crazy plan," continued Sheriff Strider, "but Eve knows her stuff. It worked. She got you to confess. Now, Dr. Tolliver, please step away from the lady. I'm a very good shot but sadly I never get the opportunity to prove it in the field. I suggest not giving me that opportunity."

"This is entrapment!" Reid exclaimed.

The sheriff responded with a lengthy explanation that Reid had the right to remain silent while Olive delighted in being given handcuffing privileges.

.

## Chapter Twenty-Seven

In the next few gloriously uneventful days, the warm Arizona sun had taken its rightful place in the sky, melted the snow, and dried the mud. Just like the sun, Eve had fallen back into her normal routine as well. The drama of the conference was beginning to seem like a distant memory— until Naiya insisted on bringing it up. Eve was happy to see Naiya who had come for a routine check-up on the horses. They hadn't seen each other since the snow melted and Eve was satisfied to see that her friend was back to her old self. Crying Naiya had been replaced by regular Confident Naiya. She had finished the check up and she and Eve were on the front porch watching the sunset and catching up.

"I'm taking the sheriff's side on this one," said Naiya. "That plan was crazy."

"It worked," Eve said defensively.

"But it had so many moving parts. There must have been an easier way."

"You know I don't like things to be too easy," Eve said with a laugh. "The more work the more fun, right? Isn't that why we're friends?"

"I'm starting to question that theory. I'm starting to think easier is easier. It's a good thing you kept me in the dark because I wouldn't have let you do it. I still can't believe the sheriff went along with it. I mean, seriously. You had Loretta drive out to the winery to make tracks in the snow so it wouldn't be so obvious that there were also the Sheriff's tire tracks?"

"The snow presented a problem," said Eve. "I needed Loretta to take Ramon out there and Olive was spying on me and overheard our conversation about setting up a recording device, so I included her. So, Loretta's drive accomplished multiple things. She made there and back tracks to behind the building so the sheriff could use the same route and hide his vehicle. She also took Ramon and Olive to the winery and, by the way, she did bring some cases of needed wine to the hotel."

"Why couldn't you have done it somewhere in the hotel?" Naiya said.

"I needed Reid to feel safe to talk. I needed him to think his plan of pinning the murder on Margo worked. I needed him away from all the eavesdropping busybodies in the hotel so he would feel comfortable enough to confess. It would have been harder to keep everyone away here at the hotel."

"There had to be an easier way," Naiya insisted.

"I had to come up with something quickly! Deputy Navarro had picked up Margo, but she wasn't talking. Sheriff Strider thought that must mean Margo was indeed guilty of killing Art, but I had my theory that it was Reid. I thought using his interest in me was my best way to see if I was right."

"And that whole 'Margo has disappeared!' thing was all for show."

"Well," Eve said with a little embarrassment, "I thought if the sheriff and I staged a scene showing that we were both sure that Margo was guilty, Reid would relax. And I thought if we argued and I seemed upset;

Reid would be happy to be my shoulder to cry on. Then I thought I could pretend to be on his side to get him to confess, which he would feel more comfortable doing if he thought we were completely alone. And if I was right, I wanted his confession recorded. It was a good plan. It worked!"

Naiya pursed her lips and shook her head.

Eve thought she should be getting kudos not criticism. She kind of missed Crying Naiya. Confident Naiya was a little judgmental. Eve was annoyed and decided she'd return the favor. "I heard that Dr. Burt poached a few more of your clients," Eve said with trepidation, since she had reconsidered her mean-spirited subject change halfway through the sentence.

"Oh, yeah. He did," Naiya replied casually.

Eve was happy to see that she hadn't succeeded in upsetting her friend, but she was confused. She raised an eyebrow as she said, "You don't care anymore?"

"It's kind of nice having a little more free time. I think I was more overworked than I realized. It's liberating to know that I'm not the only one responsible for all the animals in the area."

"But aren't you losing money?"

"Not anymore."

"How is that?"

"Burt is renting the cabin on my property."

"What?"

"And he's helping out at the office, and with the boarding facility."

"What?" Eve shook her head. "Your nemesis?"

"Nemesis? Don't be ridiculous."

"Dr. Burt is working with you?"

"I just call him Burt, but yes. It's only been a few days, but it's working out really nicely."

"Really? I don't understand. How did all this happen in just a few days?"

"I don't know. It just did and it was easy. Hence my

new outlook on life. Easy is easier. I'm just going with it."

"Really?" Eve repeated. "What about his dodgy secretive nature?"

"Oh, he told me all about that. He was being secretive about his job in Kentucky because he anonymously turned them in for inhumane practices. The longer he worked for them, the more he learned and saw, the more ill he felt working for them. But he was under an iron clad contract and couldn't quit. That's why he started volunteering at CARED. He couldn't leave his job, but at least he could try to do some good during his free time. And at work, he started gathering up damning evidence to use against them. At the end of his contract, he used all of the information he had collected on the Worthington Collective to report them. He was instructed to keep a low profile and talk as little as possible about his involvement with the organization while the investigation is ongoing."

"You just completely trust him now?"

"Yes. I do. I really do. It's been great. If it continues to go this well, who knows, maybe we'll go into business together."

"How… Why…?"

"Things change," Naiya said with a coy smile. "Sometimes they change for the better and sometimes it's best not to question why."

"Oh," Eve said with understanding. "I get it."

"You get what?"

"This is huge. You like him. I mean LIKE like him."

"There you go, getting all 12-years-old on me again."

"Deflection."

"That reminds me…" Naiya said as she reached into her bag. She pulled out a keychain and handed it to Eve. "I finally got the spare keys to the winery made."

Eve took the keys and noticed the unmistakable shape of the keychain: a half heart with jagged edges in the middle. It read "BEST."

Eve laughed. "Seriously?"

"They were in the selection at the general store," said Naiya as she watched a vehicle coming up the long driveway to the hotel. "I couldn't help myself. And this way, we'll know whose keys are whose. You're 'Best' and I'm 'Friends.'"

"Another thing you are, is not done telling me about Burt."

Naiya pointed to the approaching truck pulling up in the circle drive in front of the hotel. "Oh, look who's here. Saved by the sheriff." Naiya gathered her things together and stood to leave.

The sheriff parked his personal vehicle in front of the hotel and exited the truck wearing his civilian clothes. Naiya walked down the porch steps with a backwards wave and a, "Toodles."

"I thought you were staying for dinner," Eve uselessly called after Naiya as she walked by the sheriff and gave him a nod of greeting and goodbye.

When Sheriff Strider reached Eve, he said, "She looked suspicious. Should I arrest her?"

"Definitely. But let me be the one to question her."

After his polite chuckle, he became serious. "So, I'm just going to come out and say it." He took a deep breath. "I think you are amazing."

"Finally! I didn't realize brainwashing took so long," she blurted out with a smile.

"It didn't take long. It just took me a long time to say it out loud."

Eve felt her sassiness slip away as self-consciousness took over. "Oh," she squeaked.

"Would you like to go out with me?" he asked. When Eve silently stared at him like a deer in headlights for a socially unacceptable amount of time, he added, "Is that a no?"

She finally forced words to come out of her mouth. "A date?"

"Yes. Will you go on a date with me?"

"I…" she sort of said.

"You can just say 'no,' or preferably something nicer like 'no thank you.'"

"I'm sorry. It's not you, it's dates, first dates really. They're so awkward."

"I don't know that they're any more awkward than this conversation."

Eve laughed nervously. "True. They're like this conversation but much longer. After all, you were witness to my last first date. See how that worked out for Reid? Pretty bad, right? Are you sure you want to join that club?"

The sheriff shook his head in response to her shirk. "What specifically do you hate about first dates?"

"First dates are filled with uncomfortable questions, embarrassing new scenarios, awkward hesitations, unanticipated snags. It's rough. And you have all the nervousness leading up to the date which just makes it worse."

"Will you go on a second date with me?"

Her face softened as she took a breath. "I would love to go on a second date with you," she said with feeling. "But how can we skip the first one?"

"I have an idea. Wait here."

Eve knew that the sheriff— who she now was supposed to call Keith? That was weird— was only in the hotel for five minutes, but it felt like it was forever. She didn't know what to do with herself and didn't know what he was doing or if he had snuck out the back door and she would never see him again. She felt like an insecure teenager, another symptom of first dates.

She was about to barge in the front door and look for him when he came out of the hotel and presented his arm to her. "M'lady."

"M'lady?"

"Wrong choice of words, check," he laughed. "Will you take my arm so I can escort you in?"

Eve was in a haze of confusion. "Take your arm?"

He took her limp arm and intertwined it in his. "Awkard physical engagement. Check. I'll go ahead and double down on that one." He quickly leaned in and gave her a quick kiss on the cheek. "I made reservations inside." He opened the door, guiding her into the hotel in her trancelike state. They walked into the dining room that was sparsely inhabited by hotel guests having dinner and then to the table in the corner which uncharacteristically featured her antique silver candlestick holders on it holding lit tapered candles. "Should I pull out the chair for you or would that be weird?"

Comprehension finally caught up with her. "Oh, we're doing it now?"

He smiled at her. "At least this way we don't have to have the awkward anticipation before the awkward encounter. We'll just get it out of the way and look forward to our second date."

Keith— Eve once again reminded herself that you can't call your date "Sheriff" — pulled out the chair for her and added an embarrassing bow.

"Weird," Eve said, answering his earlier question. "Definitely weird. Don't pull out a chair for me. Or at least, lose the bow."

"Noted," he said with a smile.

After they both sat, Roxie walked into the room and up to their table. "Welcome, you two lovebirds. My name is Roxie. I'll be your server tonight."

Eve felt her cheeks warm, and she threw her face into her hands to hide the bright red spots she knew were forming on them. But it didn't take her too long to rally. She lifted her head and looked at the face of her dinner companion. She liked that face. Partly because it was the face of the man that trusted her completely. At that moment, she realized that she trusted him too. Completely. How many times had he had her back? A lot.

How many times had he let her down? Never. Yes, she trusted him completely. So, what was there to worry about?

She let herself enjoy the silliness and joy of the moment. After all, there were some benefits to feeling like a teenager again. Change is always a little uncomfortable but, like Naiya said, sometimes things change for the better and it's best not to question why.

# Night Fall at THE ROUTE 66 RANCH HOTEL

# THE ROUTE 66 RANCH HOTEL Mystery Series

---

The escapades continue at the Route 66 Ranch Hotel, and you have a standing reservation!

Come again and join Eve and her staff for book 7, when preparations for the hotel's new wedding business turn explosive.

## Dying to Get Married at

## THE ROUTE 66 RANCH HOTEL

Printed in Dunstable, United Kingdom